Skeletons in the Closet
&
Other Creepy Stories

Cheryl Kaye Tardif

OUIJA first published in *Silver Moon Magazine*; 2004
Atrophy first published in Silver Moon Magazine; 2005
Picture Perfect first published as an Amazon Short; 2006
A Grave Error first published as an Amazon Short, 2006
Remote Control - first published as a novelette in July 2010; finalist in 2008 Textnovel Contest

http://www.cherylktardif.com

FIRST EDITION

Imajin Books - www.imajinbooks.com

ISBN: 978-1-926997-05-6

eBook editions also available at various ebook retailers

Cover Design: Sapphire Designs - http://www.designs.sapphiredreams.org

Novels by Cheryl Kaye Tardif

Whale Song
The River
Children of the Fog

Series by Cheryl Kaye Tardif

The Divine Series:
Divine Intervention
Divine Justice*

Short Stories by Cheryl Kaye Tardif

Remote Control
Skeletons in the Closet & Other Creepy Stories

Novels by Cherish D'Angelo (aka Cheryl Kaye Tardif)

Lancelot's Lady

*Coming soon!

**For my dear friend Betty Dravis,
author extraordinaire and celebrity interviewer**

Betty, you are a super star and I am blessed to know you.

Enter the closet...

We *all* have skeletons in our closets.
Some are just more alive than others.
~ *Cheryl Kaye Tardif*

Introduction

Ever since I was a young girl, I've loved short, scary stories that made me quiver with anticipation and fear. My author idol, Stephen King, gave me more sleepless nights and nightmares than I can count, and yet I gobbled up every book he wrote. I spent many nights waiting for my breathing to calm and my heart to stop racing. It was exhilarating!

Skeletons in the Closet & Other Creepy Stories has been a dream of mine since I was about 16, and I'm excited to be able to share it with you. It contains some works that are based on stories I wrote almost 25 years ago.

Remote Control was originally written as an assignment about irony for a Journalism and Short Story Writing course I took after high-school. Separation Anxiety is an older story that delves into themes of loss, death and irony. Atrophy came out of the darkest corner of my mind, one that's a bit twisted. Sweet Dreams is a story I wrote for a writer's group contest in which we had to write something that reflected a photograph of a wooded, isolated area with gloomy lighting. I won.

The three Myrtle Murphy Mysteries feature an elderly serial killer you'll hate to love. My writers' group assigned three words to incorporate into a story for the first two Mysteries. Picture Perfect is one of my personal favorite short stories. It's a supernatural short about sisterly love and envy. Ouija and The Car are based on true events. Believe it or don't.

1

Caller Unknown, Deadly Reunion and Skeletons in the Closet are shorts that have never before been published or online.

My greatest desire is to get your heart pounding, to make you jump when you hear a strange sound, and to give you at least one sleepless night. If I accomplish any of these, then I've done my job. ☺

Cheryl Kaye Tardif
July 2010

A Grave Error

(Myrtle Murphy Mystery #1)

Myrtle Murphy had everything she wanted out of life—a dead husband, a grown son who'd moved to the opposite coast and neighbors who minded their own business. But what she didn't have was money. She needed a job. At sixty-one and living off a pittance of an early retirement pension, she had no skills to fall back on.

Unless you could call slipping your husband small doses of rat poison in his evening tea for over a month a skill. Yet, on the other hand, it *had* taken a certain amount of talent to flavor the tea—*just so*—to avoid being caught. And it had definitely taken a particular cleverness to dispose of Norman's body.

Norm.

Now there was a waste of space.

Ever since he decided to have a midlife crisis at forty-eight, the man had been virtually useless. And yes, *he* decided. That's exactly what he told her after he came home with a brand new sports car that they couldn't afford.

"I'm having a midlife crisis, Myrt, and you better get used to it."

After that he started going out with the 'boys'.

Boys! Yeah, right!

The 'boys' were three semi-retired old coots, like Norm, who had nothing better to do than sit around Farley's Pub and get drunk, while spending their paychecks at the slot machines. Sometimes she'd find one of boys passed out on her couch the next morning. Often there was a mess of vomit on the floor.

And who do you suppose cleaned that up?

Myrtle, of course.

For a while, she considered having her own midlife crisis, maybe buy herself a sports car, or go to a club for ladies' night. But she knew she was well past all that nonsense.

Myrtle was having a Norman crisis instead.

Her husband of thirty odd years was always complaining about how his life could have been better if he had done *this*. Or become *that*. Or lived *there*. He had practically driven her around the bend with his constant complaining.

"I should've gone into computers," he muttered one day while they were dining at Denny's. "That's where the money is."

"That's what you said last week about banking," she said dryly. "Why can't you just be happy with being a plumber? Some of your friends make more than enough." She paused, stroking her chin in mock thoughtfulness. "Course, they work twice as much as you do, and they don't turn down jobs because their thumb hurts."

"Well, it did," he argued.

She rolled her eyes. "And what about the time you said no to the townhouse complex, just because you wanted to go to the races with your *boys*?"

"I needed a couple of days off," he said belligerently. "I worked hard that week."

She snorted.

"What?" he demanded. "What do *you* do all day? Watch soap operas is my guess."

Her eyes narrowed. "You mean, what do I do after I've cleaned the house, washed all the laundry, paid our bills, checked the mail, gone shopping and made dinner? Hmm, well since you've been getting home around three each day, that doesn't leave me much time to watch soap operas, now does it?"

The waitress interrupted them with their meals, a chicken salad for Myrtle and a bacon cheeseburger with fries for Norm. The girl plopped a bottle of ketchup on the table, then asked if they needed anything else.

How about a cattle prod? Myrtle was tempted to say.

"Oh, by the way," Norm said when the girl had left. "I'm gonna take back that vest you bought me."

Her brow arched. "Really."

He was talking about the green plaid vest she'd gotten him for his birthday last week. The one he had practically begged her for, that she'd traipsed three malls to find.

"Yeah," he continued. "The boys said it washed me out, made me look old. Said I'd look better in red."

4

She was about to make a sarcastic remark when Norm got to his feet.

"Be right back," he said, before disappearing into the washroom.

She picked up her fork, but her gaze came to rest on the ketchup bottle. It was the glass kind, the one with the little twist-off cap. The kind that was always temperamental, that wouldn't release the ketchup, forcing you to—

A monsoon of an idea washed over her.

She covertly glanced around the restaurant, then eyed the bathroom door. Quickly, before she could change her mind, she loosened the cap on the ketchup bottle. Then she slid the bottle toward her husband's plate, knowing that he wouldn't resist having ketchup with his fries.

Sure enough, as soon as he sat down, he gripped the bottle in one hand.

She held her breath, waiting to see him upend it all over his meal.

But that's not exactly what happened.

What *did* happen was far more rewarding.

Norm shook the bottle. Vigorously.

The cap flew off and ketchup exploded everywhere. It coated his gray hair, his grizzled face, then slid down his throat and under the collar of his white shirt. The shocked look in his eyes swiftly turned to embarrassment.

Myrtle passed him a napkin. "You should always check the lid first."

A dribble of red goo oozed down Norm's shirt and plopped into his lap.

"I'll go clean up in the bathroom," he mumbled.

When he was almost at the bathroom door, she couldn't resist a last dig.

"The boys were right," she hollered.

Heads turned. People gasped, pointed and laughed.

"About what?" Norm snapped.

She grinned. "You do look better in red."

That night, her husband went on a rampage. He didn't outright accuse her of loosening the ketchup cap, but she could see it in his eyes. He suspected her.

"You better wash my shirt right away," he insisted. "I don't want it to stain."

"Wash it yourself," she said with a scowl.

"I can't. My back hurts."

Her mouth thinned in anger.

If it wasn't his back bothering him, it was his leg. Or he had indigestion, or his eye was twitching, or his ear was itchy.

"If it gets worse I won't be able to go to work tomorrow," he said slyly.

She washed the shirt. And left out the fabric softener.

* * *

The next night, Norm continued his little game. This time he had a migraine.

That was the moment she snapped.

"You're giving *me* a migraine!" she yelled.

"Shh," Norm moaned, cringing and squinting up at her. "Make me some tea, will ya." It wasn't a request.

She glared at him, hands on hips, fuming. *Sometimes you're such a pest, Norm.*

A slow smile emerged. "Sure thing…*dear*."

The rat poison was tucked under the kitchen sink, way in the back. She'd found it the other day when she was looking for a scrub brush. She had no idea where the box had come from. She hadn't even known they had a rat problem.

"One half teaspoon," she murmured, carefully measuring out the fine white powder.

A sprinkle of cinnamon and a spoonful of honey made Norm's tea just right. At least she hoped so. She certainly wasn't going to taste it to make sure.

"Here," she said, plopping the cup down on the coffee table. "And here's a wedge of lemon."

She studied him, a bit like a scientist studies a lab rat just before he administers something deadly. When Norm squeezed the lemon into his tea, she walked away, pleased by his inadvert assistance.

That night in bed, her poor husband couldn't sleep.

"I have a tummy ache, Myrt," he whimpered.

Tummy? What grown man said 'tummy'?

"Must be something you ate," she said, rolling away from him so he wouldn't see her grin.

* * *

The following night, she made his evening tea with its special ingredient. She did this every day afterward. After a week, Norm began complaining that his vision was blurry.

Myrtle told him to get new glasses.

Then she upped the rat poison to one teaspoon.

This went on for just over a month—until the night Norman Murphy did something phenomenal. He dropped dead.

6

Actually, it wasn't so much a *drop*, more like a *crash*. And a *splatter*.

It happened while she was sitting on the couch, watching House. Norm went into the kitchen and brought back a pitcher of orange juice. He was standing right in front of her, about to set it on the coffee table, when he let out a tortured groan. The pitcher flew out of his hands and juice erupted into the air.

Unfortunately, Myrtle wore it. From the top of her head, down to her toes.

"For heaven's sake!" she sputtered. "Watch what you're—"

Norm hit the floor. He slid, face-first, until he rested at her feet.

"Norm?"

He didn't move.

She prodded him with her foot. "Hey, get up."

Still no movement.

That's when it hit her.

Norm was dead.

She cocked her juice-drenched head to the side, watching him for a long moment. She'd always wondered if she'd regret her actions, feel sorry for him, miss him, maybe even feel guilty.

"Nope," she said to his lifeless body. "Nothing."

With a shrug, she set to work on cleaning up the mess he'd made.

"Can't have a stain on the floor," she muttered. "Now can we?"

After all, it was Norm who always told her that if there was a mess in the house he expected her to take care of it. Right away.

It took almost an hour to get her husband wrapped up in an old tarp and drag him into the garage. It took another hour to clean up the orange juice and bleach the floor. After that, Myrtle had a leisurely shower, whistling all the while. Then she changed into a more practical outfit—black pants, a black turtleneck sweater and black leather gloves. She was tempted to wear Norm's black ski mask, but figured that might be overkill.

Since she'd made Norm take back the sports car the day after he brought it home, she had to settle for either his old Honda or her Mazda. Panting and straining, she inched his tarp-covered body into the trunk of the Honda. Better his car than hers.

"Shoulda gone on a diet, Norm."

With a final grunt, she heaved him into the trunk, crammed his legs inside and tossed a shovel in beside him. Letting out a satisfied sigh, she closed the trunk and drove half a mile out of the city. Finally, she veered off down a country lane, then pulled over.

7

Under a pitch black, starless midnight sky, she began to dig. Thankfully, the ground was soft, newly plowed. When the hole was deep enough, she opened the tarp and rolled Norm's body toward the edge.

"Dust to dust," she said. "Et cetera, et cetera."

She shoved him into the pit.

Norm hit the bottom with a soft thump. He landed face up, his eyes staring blindly at the sky. His left arm was bent, half-covering his chest, and one leg was twisted under him. His jumbled pose made him look like a puppet that had lost its strings.

She tossed the tarp into the grave.

An hour later, the puppet was buried.

* * *

That was almost two months ago. Now here she was, sitting at the kitchen table, scouring the classified section of the *Edmonton Sun*. She had to consider employment ads because Norm, the old coot, had forgotten to renew his life insurance policy. She should've checked into that before she decided to get rid of him.

"That was a grave error on your part, Myrtle." She doubled over in a fit of laughter. "Oh my, you're punny."

Suddenly, the doorbell rang.

With a huge grin on her face, she opened the door.

A white-haired woman in antiquated cats-eye glasses stood on the porch, looking as though she'd just stepped out of *Vogue*.

Myrtle recognized her immediately and her smile faded.

"Mother Murphy. What brings you to town?"

"I'm looking for Norman," her mother-in-law said, peering down the aquiline tip of her nose. "He hasn't called me in weeks. That's not like him."

She pushed past Myrtle and strode into the living room, her regal head swiveling back and forth as her piercing blue eyes took in every speck of dust. "Where is he?"

"He went camping with the boys." It was the first thing that came to mind.

"Camping?" Mother Murphy's lips pursed in disapproval. "When will he be back?"

Myrtle gritted her teeth. "I'm not sure. Would you like to sit for a few minutes before you head back?"

Her mother-in-law gave her the look. The one that said her son had married a moron.

"Of course I'd like to sit. Do you think I'd drive all this way just to stand here? It was a four-hour drive, in rush hour traffic, and only to find out that my son has gone…*camping*, of all things."

8

They settled in the living room, Mother Murphy in the armchair and Myrtle on the couch. For a long moment they simply watched each other. Myrtle knew the old woman was sizing her up. It's what she'd always done, ever since Norm had brought his fiancé to meet his mother.

"I wanted to let Norman know I've updated my will," her mother-in-law said finally.

Well, that was a shock. And it must have been written all over Myrtle's face because the woman continued. "Wadsworth died, and since I can no longer leave my money to my dearly departed cat, I've made Norman my beneficiary."

"Good for him."

"Of course, he probably won't see anything for a few more years. My doctor says I'm in tiptop shape." Mother Murphy gave her a chilly smile. "*You* probably won't see much of it anyway. I'm sure Norman will want to buy a new car, since you made him give his last one back." She leaned forward. "I never could understand why he married you. You're so...common."

Myrtle bristled. "Common? Your son's a plumber, for crying out loud. Not the royal heir to the throne." Her eyes narrowed. "Unless it's a toilet."

Her mother-in-law gasped, one hand raised to her throat. "Myrtle! I'm appalled." She raised her chin in defiance. "I will be speaking to Norman about this."

Myrtle hid a grin. "You do that. I don't care."

"Well, you should care," the old woman threatened. "I am his mother after all. He listens to me."

"He didn't when you told him not to marry me."

The old woman stood slowly. "I best be getting back before my neighbors wonder where I've gone."

"Didn't you tell them?" Myrtle asked, surprised.

Her mother-in-law was usually very meticulous at letting her neighbors know when she'd be gone for more than an hour. The woman was always so petrified that she'd get stuck somewhere and poor Wadsworth—a miserable, unpredictable Siamese—wouldn't get fed on time.

Correction, Myrtle. A miserable, unpredictable and now dead Siamese.

"I completely forgot to tell them," Mother Murphy admitted. "I was worried that something had happened to Norman. I know you don't look after him. He told me how you refused to wash his clothes or make his favorite meals." Her eyes iced over. "And how you watch soap operas all day."

9

At first, Myrtle said nothing. She was too busy trying to remember if there was another tarp in the garage.

She took her mother-in-law's arm and steered her back toward the living room.

"What are you doing?" the old woman demanded. "Let go of me!"

"You should rest a bit longer," Myrtle said. "You look exhausted."

"Do I?" Mother Murphy touched her face. "Perhaps I should rest. It has been a long drive. And talking to you is enough to exhaust anyone."

Myrtle smiled with saccharine sweetness. "How about I make you a nice cup of tea?"

The Death of an Old Cow

(Myrtle Murphy Mystery #2)

Myrtle Murphy had everything she wanted out of life—except her damned mother-in-law was still breathing. And that wasn't part of the plan. The bitch should have keeled over after drinking the three cups of tea laced with arsenic. Instead, she was passed out on the couch—*snoring*, of all things. And alive.

Myrtle scowled. The nerve of her!

The white-haired woman in her antiquated cats-eye glasses no longer looked like she had stepped out of *Vogue*. More like a commercial for Wrinkle-Away. Her face sagged, each crevice threatening to suck in both the foundation and blush she had caked on that morning. Her mouth was parted slightly, and every now and then she choked on a snore, her body jerking from lack of oxygen.

Myrtle shook her head in frustration. "Mother Murphy, what am I going to do with you?"

The woman had come looking for her son, but Myrtle had laid him to rest two months earlier. *Permanently.* Norman was buried in the woods, fertilizer for the voracious plants around him. He'd always said he had a green thumb.

"He hasn't called me in weeks," Mother Murphy had said when she had arrived hours ago. "That's not like him."

Myrtle had lied, told her mother-in-law that Norman had gone camping with his friends—the *"boys"*. When Mother Murphy mentioned that she had changed her will and made Norman her beneficiary since her mangy Siamese cat Wadsworth had died, Myrtle's mind started churning. And when the witch of a woman started in on her, calling her "common", Myrtle knew there was only one thing to do.

"How about I make you a nice cup of tea?" she had suggested.

11

Her mother-in-law had peered over her glasses as if Myrtle were a bug that needed to be squashed with her Gucci heel. Then she lifted her imperious chins and settled onto the sofa.

"Make it extra sweet," she commanded.

* * *

"Three cups," Myrtle muttered. "With enough of my secret ingredient to put down a cow."

She scowled at the woman. Then on impulse, she reached over and pulled the bobby pins from the woman's salon hairdo. For good measure, she mussed it up with both hands.

Myrtle stood back to admire her handiwork.

"There. You look lovely, dahling."

She had a good mind to get a tube of red lipstick and pull a Bette Davis.

Mommy Dearest.

"Now, what the hell am I going to do with you?"

She glanced at her watch. It was getting late.

The phone rang.

"Myrt, it's Harry. Is Norm back from his trip yet?"

It came out like: Myrt, is Sarry. Snorm back from strip yet?

Harry was one of the boys, and Norman's best friend. They had played football in college together. Harry called every week, usually drunk and slurring his words. Tonight was no different.

"You there, Myrtie?" he slurred. "Thought ya said he's coming back this week."

"He had to go visit his mother," Myrtle snapped. "She's sick."

She stared at the woman lying unconscious on the couch.

"Maybe dying even," she added, smiling.

"Well," Harry drawled as if it were a two-syllable word, "us boys are going to the old Morris farm and we wanted Norm to come with us."

"It's almost midnight, for God's sake," Myrtle snapped. "What the hell are you going to do out there at this time of night?"

"We's goin' cow tippin'" she heard Frank Burgess yell. Frank was Harry's twin brother and just as irritating.

Cow tipping?

Myrtle rolled her eyes and stared at the phone in her hand. Norm's friends were a waste of—

She glanced at the old woman lying on the couch and a smile crept across her face.

"The old Morris farm is just off Highway 14, right?" she asked.

12

Harry cleared his throat. "Yeah. Just let Norm know. We're getting Morris back for the stunt he played on Norm at the golf course. Okay, Myrtie?"

"Sure. I'll call him at his mother's." She hung up.

Standford Morris had been the bane of Norm's existence. A month ago at the annual senior's golf tournament, Stan had rigged the brakes on Norm's golf cart. Norm had ended up in the lake. He had always wanted to get Stan back.

An idea teased at the edge of her mind.

Her eyes widened. "Cow tipping?"

In the garage there was one vinyl tarp left, the one Norm had used to cover his sports car. She retrieved it and quickly spread it out on the floor near the couch. Then she unceremoniously rolled Mother Murphy off the edge. The woman landed with a thud, let out a soft groan, then continued her snoring. Even after Myrtle rolled her in the tarp, she remained unconscious.

Myrtle prodded the tarp with her toe, wishing she could just roll her out to the middle of the street and leave her there. But that wouldn't do. Like Norm, there had to be no evidence leading back to her.

Hunched forward, she grabbed the tarp and heaved it, stepping backwards bit by bit. By the time she reached the garage door she was covered in sweat.

"You certainly weigh a lot, Mother Murphy. You're just a fat old cow."

Straightening, she chuckled and brushed her limp bangs from her forehead. Then she continued to haul the tarp-covered body down the three steps to the garage.

Thunk, thunk, thunk!

Her mother-in-law would have a headache…if she ever woke up.

Resting for a moment, Myrtle leaned against the car, considering her idea. If it worked, the police would never suspect her. They'd have other suspects to question.

Another ten minutes and Mother Murphy was securely dumped into the trunk of Norm's car. Then Myrtle set off toward Highway 14.

* * *

"Ah, I see you guys," she murmured as she killed the headlights and slowed the car to a crawl.

Under a pitch-black, moonless sky, she passed by the dirt road where Harry had parked his car. Up ahead, another dirt road was unimpeded by parked vehicles so she pulled off and stopped the car. A quick reconnaissance of the area showed that the boys were still in Harry's car, probably polishing off a case of Old Milwaukee. Small red lights flickered inside. The boys were smoking up a storm, and she guessed they weren't all cigarettes.

"Let's go for a walk, Mother."

She popped the trunk and hefted the tarp over the side. It slid to the hard, dry ground. Grabbing the edge, she began pulling it into the field, pausing every now and then to catch her breath.

She had worn Norm's old gum boots, and although they were far too big, she figured the treads would never lead the police to her door. They'd be looking for a man with size eleven boots. And she'd be sure to dispose of them on her way home.

She stopped suddenly and held her breath.

A motionless shadow blocked her way.

It took her a moment to realize it was a blasted cow. The only cow in the field.

Perfect!

She positioned Mother Murphy alongside the sleeping cow, careful not to make any sudden moves or sounds. Even the old bat was agreeably quiet, her snoring disappearing altogether. Myrtle was tempted to unroll the tarp. Maybe her mother-in-law had suffocated.

A door slammed.

Crouching low, she peered under the cow's belly, her eyes seeking the car.

Harry, Frank and two other men moved stealthily across the field.

Time to move, Myrtle.

As she moved away and headed into the bushes, she glanced back. There was a bare hump in the grass where Mother Murphy lay sleeping. The cow stood stock-still next to her.

From the vantage point of the bushes, Myrtle could barely contain her glee. The boys were loaded. They'd never notice the tarp, even if they tripped over it.

She heard faint snickers. Then someone shushed the others.

After that everything happened in slow motion. It was almost like she'd been teleported back to the last college football game, where Harry had scored the winning touchdown. In a single fluid movement, the four beefy men ran at the cow, their arms stretched, making no sounds. Until they hit the cow.

Thwack!

"Tackle!" Harry shouted.

In the same instant, the cow went down, waking suddenly and letting out a startled moo. But the momentum of the men toppled it and the cow hit the ground—and the tarp containing Mother Murphy—with a sickening splat that seemed to reverberate through the night.

14

The men cackled with intoxicated amusement.

"Let's get outta here," Frank slurred. "My shoes are covered in shit."

"Gawd almighty," Frank said. "Can't believe we did it."

"Yeah, that old cow must be deader than ground beef," one of the other men said.

Myrtle stifled a laugh, then sneaked back to her car.

On the ride home, she couldn't help but think of that last comment.

"That old cow must be deader than ground beef," she mimicked. "Yep, she sure must be."

Myrtle Murphy had only two things left to do. She'd dump the gum boots in a trash bin on the way home. And she'd pick up a cheeseburger at Burger King. She had a sudden craving for beef.

Maid of Dishonor

(Myrtle Murphy Mystery #3)

Myrtle Murphy thought she had everything out of life, like a dead husband buried in the woods and a mother-in-law thankfully flattened by a sleeping cow. However, she began to feel rather lonely. After all, now that Norm was gone, the house was deathly quiet. So quiet that even her breathing seemed to echo down the hallway of the dreary two-story Victorian home. And there was an emptiness that pervaded each room, as if every molecule of oxygen had been vaporized and replaced with a void of stale, shadowed nothingness.

Like a tomb, Myrtle thought one day. And there's no Harrison Ford coming to my rescue.

It was time to do something about it.

She picked up the phone and carefully flicked through the Rolodex. No telling who's in here.

Her hand paused suddenly. "Rick Ferelli? Well, lordy, how did that get in here?"

She plucked out the small rectangular card and squinted. She recognized Norm's handwriting immediately. But what the hell was he doing with her sister's ex-husband's phone number?

Good God, did Norm find out what I did?

Her wrinkled hand crept to her throat as she recalled the catastrophe that was her sister's wedding day thirty-five years ago...

* * *

"Are you ready yet, Myrtle Anne?" her mother shouted, pounding on the bathroom door. "You know, other people could use the mirror more than you."

Myrtle adjusted the blue satin dress and twirled in the mirror, admiring her new hairdo. Turning her head to examine her profile, she couldn't help but notice how closely she resembled Eliza, her sister. Eliza

16

was getting married in a few hours, and thank God she had the brains to order decent dresses for her bridesmaids and maid of honor.

"I should've been her maid of honor," she muttered.

Myrtle was still hurt by the fact that Eliza had chosen her best friend for the highest honor. How could Eliza do this to her?

"Always a bridesmaid," Myrtle said to her reflection.

Just that morning, her mother had warned her that she'd better hurry up and get married if she wanted children. She'd just turned twenty-six. A spinster, by her mother's terms.

"For crying out loud, your sister who is six years younger than you is getting married before you. What's wrong with you, Myrtle Anne? Why can't you find a man?"

Myrtle frowned in the mirror. *I did find a man, Mother.*

Unfortunately, Eliza had beaten her to him.

Rick...

Ricardo Ferelli was a young legal assistant when Myrtle had first met him. Tall, handsome, with a mind bent on a career as an attorney, he had all the qualities she was looking for. They'd gone out for six months when he finally convinced her to invite him to dinner at her family home in Sherwood Park. Her mother had been more than thrilled.

So was Myrtle. Things were looking serious. She'd finally found her man—until Rick set eyes on Eliza.

Although Ricardo Ferelli had swept into both of their lives, he'd been swept out of Myrtle's faster than she could say "I do." In fact, she never even had the chance to contemplate those words. Eliza would be saying them instead.

Myrtle glanced at her watch. It was nearing 7:00 PM.

Almost time to leave for the church.

She emerged from the bathroom, ignored her mother and headed downstairs. From the top step, she could see a small group of women standing in the living room. Eliza was in the center, all bride-like and glowing in her form-fitting, white satin wedding dress with the tiny diamonds on the bodice. Beside her stood Stephanie, her maid of honor and best friend.

Myrtle's face transformed into a hardened mask of anger and jealousy. *Eliza, you traitor!* Resentment boiled with each step, threatening to erupt like a bad case of acid reflux. In that moment, she didn't know who she hated more, Stephanie or her own sister.

"Myrtle!" her sister exclaimed over the loud music. "I was wondering where you were."

Like you really care, Myrtle wanted to say.

She glared at Stephanie. "How come everyone's inside?"

17

Eliza pouted, something she was very good at. "It's raining."

Myrtle glanced out the window. Sure enough, a light drizzle watered the yard and disturbed the dark surface of the barely visible swimming pool.

"Your mom forgot to buy new bulbs for the outdoor lights," Stephanie said. "If it wasn't raining we'd have drinks by the pool before the wedding."

Myrtle's brow arched. "Looks like you've already had a few."

Stephanie gave her an overstretched smile. "One glass of wine."

Eliza grabbed Myrtle's arm and dragged her into an alcove. "What are you doing? This is my wedding day."

"Yes, it is." But it should have been mine!

"Look, Myrt, you told me you understood when I told you I wanted Stephanie to be my maid of honor. She's my best friend."

I understand that you're thoughtless. "I do understand. I just don't like her." At Eliza's shocked expression Myrtle added, "So sue me."

Thankfully, their mother interrupted them. "We're popping open a bottle of champagne in the kitchen." She took Eliza's arm and whisked her away.

Myrtle hung back, tempted to ditch the wedding and head for a bar where she could get seriously drunk.

"Where is everyone?" Stephanie asked.

Myrtle eyed her for a moment, then shrugged. "Don't know."

"Can you tell your sister I'm moving my car to the grocery store parking lot out front?" Stephanie pulled her car keys from a silver handbag. "I'm in the alley and I don't want to be towed."

"It's dark out there. I'll come with you."

In hindsight, if Myrtle had paused to think about her unusual offer, she would have realized that a plan had started to percolate.

* * *

Myrtle snuck a peek in the foyer mirror. A strand of hair was dislodged and she tucked it back behind a hairpin.

"We're getting ready to go," her mother told her. "I'll take Aunt Lucy and the bridesmaids. You're okay to drive your sister and Stephanie?"

"Of course. I only had a rum and Coke." *Hold the Coke.*

Myrtle helped Eliza into the backseat.

"Where's Stephanie?"

Myrtle shrugged. "She said something about her car."

"What do you mean? She's parked out back."

"I know," Myrtle said. "She had her keys out. She must have thought there wasn't enough room."

Eliza blew out a breath of relief. "So she's meeting us at the church." She laughed. "For a minute I was worried."

"Yeah, can't have a missing maid of honor, now can we?"

Eliza shook her head. Then she took Myrtle's hand. "I'm so glad you understand, sis. I didn't want you mad at me on my wedding day."

Myrtle painted on a smile. "Now why would I be mad at you?"

She was about to close the car door, when her sister let out a loud gasp. "My dress!"

Eliza hauled in handfuls of fabric just in time.

Myrtle swore beneath her breath.

* * *

"Where can she be?" Eliza asked for the millionth time. Her voice crackled with unshed tears. "She should have been here before us."

"I'm sure Stephanie will be here any minute, dear," their mother said, stroking Eliza's arm.

Everyone was in a panic over Stephanie. Everyone, that is, except for Myrtle. She played the concerned sister and called Stephanie's number. She even left messages.

"Stephanie, it's Myrtle. We're all at the church. Where are you?"

Eliza moaned. "What am I going to do, Mom? She's my maid of honor."

"Maybe she's here but doesn't know what room we're in. I'll go check, dear."

Myrtle watched their mother scurry off in the direction of the church entrance.

"Oh, Myrtle," Eliza wailed. "Stephanie was supposed to help me get ready."

Myrtle turned her toward the floor length mirror. "I think I did a pretty good job."

"Tell me what Stephanie said to you again."

Myrtle let out an irritated sigh. "She had her keys in her hand and said she was going out to her car. I thought she was driving here."

"And Mom checked the alley?"

"That's what she said. And there was no sign of Stephanie's car."

A tear trickled down her sister's face. "Then where is she?"

"Maybe she stopped off at her boyfriend's house."

Eliza's mouth opened, then closed. "She doesn't have a boyfriend."

"Maybe she went to a pub for a few more drinks," Myrtle said, her voice hardening.

"She wouldn't do that." Her sister stared up at her. "Why do you always have to be so mean? Stephanie's never done anything to you."

Myrtle clamped her lips tight. No, nothing except take my place as your maid of honor.

"Look, Eliza, I have no idea why your *best friend* would go traipsing off somewhere when she knows you're getting married." Myrtle glanced at her watch, "You're already twenty minutes late."

"I can't get married without Stephanie!"

"Of course you can. Rick's waiting for you." *And you wouldn't want to keep him waiting.*

"You're right," her sister said between her tears. She turned back to the mirror. "Now help me fix my makeup. I want to be perfect for Rickie."

"Rickie?" Good God.

In the mirror, Eliza's eyes widened. "Shh, don't tell him I told you. I'm the only one who calls him that."

"Maybe because he's a grown man."

"No, silly. It's his *special* name." Eliza lowered her voice to a whisper. "You know, for when we do it."

Suddenly, Myrtle was slammed with a terrible image, an image of Eliza wrapped in Rick's strong arms as they made love. The acid reflux that had boiled earlier rose to the back of her throat. She grabbed her throat, coaxing it back down, but not before contemplating spewing fiery black acid all over her sister's pure white dress.

"I know," Eliza said with a giggle. "Too much information."

In reply, Myrtle cinched in the ties at the back of Eliza's dress.

"That's a little tight, sis. I can barely breathe."

Don't tempt me, dear sister.

Their mother waltzed into the room. "It's time!" She gave Myrtle a quick peck on the cheek, then wrapped her arms around Eliza. "My baby's getting married."

Eliza smiled brightly. "Oh, Mom. I'm not a baby anymore."

The three of them bustled out of the room, Myrtle taking up the rear, while Eliza and their mother held hands and giggled like school kids. Myrtle scowled and took an extra long stride, stepping on the train of Eliza's dress.

"Be careful, Myrtle!" their mother scolded. "You don't want to ruin Eliza's beautiful dress."

Maybe I do, Mother.

The pastor hurried toward them. "Are you all set?"

Eliza took a deep breath. "My maid of honor isn't here yet."

"That's a shame," the pastor said. "We're just going to have to start without her." He smiled, oblivious to Eliza's distress. "At least the bride and groom are here."

"Can't we wait another half hour?" Eliza begged.

The pastor gave her an apologetic smile. "We're already late, my dear. I have an appointment in another hour." He glanced at Myrtle. "I'm sure your sister wouldn't mind standing in as your maid of honor."

His comment made Myrtle grin. "Of course I can stand in for Stephanie," she said, as if it hadn't crossed her mind. "Come on, Eliza. It's time for you to get married."

* * *

The wedding ceremony went smoothly. Myrtle had stood beside her sister, held the bride's lush bouquet, and whispered the vows while smiling into the eyes of the groom.

The bastard never even noticed her.

That's when Myrtle came up with another plan.

Once the reception at the Holiday Inn was underway and everyone was feeling the effects of too much champagne, she slipped a note in Rick's tuxedo pocket. Fifteen minutes later, she saw him pull it out, read it, then smirk with glee.

He gave his bride a wink, then headed toward the bar.

Rushing towards her sister, Myrtle said, "I think I saw Stephanie's car in the parking lot."

Eliza's eyes lit up. "Really?"

Myrtle nodded. "I'm pretty sure it's hers."

Eliza bunched up the sides of her dress and hurried from the reception hall. Across the room, Rick grinned.

Within seconds, Myrtle was running to the elevator, a room key card in hand. She'd taken it from her sister's purse earlier in the evening.

Inside room 403, she briefly took in the honeymoon suite with its heart-shaped bed, chilled champagne, red roses and chocolate covered strawberries. Then she stripped naked. Hanging her dress up in the closet, she turned off all the lights and slid between the silky sheets.

Anticipation teased her body until she was ready to explode.

Finally, she heard a card slide in the door. It opened, silhouetting Rick's tall frame for a second. He quickly shut the door.

"Lizzie, you're a wicked girl," Rick's shadow said in the dark. "When I got your note telling me you would be waiting for me here in the dark, I thought, 'What would your mother think?' He chuckled. "Then I realized I didn't care. I want to make love to you until you scream, my lovely wife."

Sounds of clothes being tossed on the chair were followed by movement on the bed. In a flash, hot hands slid over Myrtle's body. She bit her lip to keep from moaning.

"Lizzie..."

Rick's tongue slid into her mouth. She ravenously kissed him back. It had been a long time since she'd had sex. Over a year. He'd been the last one…her *only* one.

"Rickie," she whispered against his mouth.

His fingers danced down her body, sending shivers of excitement through her veins. Then his lips trailed butterfly kisses down her neck to her breasts.

Would he notice she was smaller than her sister?

No, poor Rickie didn't notice a thing.

Not even later when she cried out in ecstasy.

Afterward, Rick dressed in the dark, just as she'd instructed him in her note. He kissed her lips. "I'll see you downstairs, my love."

As soon as the door closed behind him, Myrtle let out a heavy breath. Good God, the man could screw. She could've gone another round.

Stretching like a cat, she giggled. "Happy wedding night, Rick."

She dressed slowly, as if in a dream, then left the honeymoon suite, feeling more bride-like than she could ever imagine. Plucking a chocolate strawberry from the platter, she bit into it and moaned with pleasure. It was almost as delicious as the orgasm Rick had given her.

Almost.

The elevator took her down to the lobby level. She entered the reception hall just in time to see Rick crossing the room. A sea of wedding guests parted and there was Lizzie in all her bridal glory stepping inside through the exit door to the parking lot.

Rick lurched to a stop. He glanced around the room, a look of horror plastered on his face. Myrtle could almost hear his thoughts. *What was Lizzie doing outside? Wait! She couldn't have made it downstairs before me. I left first.* His horrified expression turned sickly. *Oh my God. What have I done? Who was that upstairs?*

Myrtle took a step forward, then paused when Rick's gaze found hers. The smile she gave him started slowly, two tugs on the corners of her mouth. It then grew into a wide, knowing smile.

Thanks, Rick.

His face now paler than a corpse, he approached her, every expression churning in his dark eyes. Regret, sorrow, anger, fear.

It was the latter that made Myrtle laugh out loud.

Rick reached her. "What have you done?"

She batted her eyes at him. "I have no idea what you're talking about." With that, she whirled away, heading toward her sister.

"Myrtle, can you believe it?" Eliza said, flashing her rings. "I'm married."

"Let's hope you can stay married," Myrtle muttered.

"How can you say that?"

"You know men. They're fickle to the core."

Almost as fickle as my sister.

"Not Rick," Eliza argued. "He's loyal to the core. He'd never cheat on me."

Myrtle glanced over her shoulder. Rick was a few steps away, but by the look on his face, he'd caught Eliza's declaration.

"Never, Eliza?" she said, grinning. "You know what they say. Never say never."

"Where have you been?" Eliza asked her new husband.

"I, uh…" Rick glared at Myrtle. "I have to go ask your mother something. I'll be right back."

"We're going to talk about this," Rick whispered as he passed by.

Myrtle didn't know if he meant they'd talk or he'd talk with Eliza. Either way it didn't matter to her. *What's done is done.* She wouldn't take back a minute of Rick's body on hers, inside her, for anything.

"I couldn't find Stephanie anywhere," Eliza said, tugging on her arm.

"I'm sorry, sis. I thought it was her. Hasn't she called you?"

Eliza shook her head.

"Did you call her?"

"At least a half dozen times," Eliza said. "I think something's happened to her."

"You mean like she got in a car accident or something?"

Eliza nodded. "Or got a flat tire. And maybe her car phone is dead. She always forgets to charge it. And she probably left all her credit cards at home, since everything was free tonight. She never likes to carry a heavy purse." She paused. "I never did thank you, Myrtle, for stepping in as my maid of honor."

"My pleasure." Myrtle awkwardly patted her sister's shoulder, hoping it resembled something a concerned sister would do. "I'm sure your real maid of honor will turn up today or tomorrow.

* * *

Stephanie did turn up, just as Myrtle had predicted.

The morning after Eliza's wedding, their mother had taken her morning tea and toast outside. She planned on having breakfast while sitting in her favorite wicker chair near the pool. Breakfast, however, was put on hold so she could call 911 and report the dead body floating in her swimming pool.

"You should have seen S-Stephanie," she sobbed to Myrtle and Eliza. "The poor girl must have slipped and hit her head on the edge of the pool." Sob. "Then her lovely maid of honor dress weighted her down."

"The poor girl indeed," Myrtle said, shaking her head slowly.

It took a lot of composure to not burst out laughing.

* * *

Myrtle Murphy was known for her calm composure and demeanor in the face of adversity. This ability had come in handy over the years. It had gotten her through a terrible marriage, and her husband's untimely disappearance. The police still hadn't found his body. It had even gotten her through dealing with Mother Murphy, a grand matriarch with a firm handshake and a weakness for tea.

She stared now at the small piece of paper in her hand.

Rick Ferelli. Her sister's ex-husband, now turned attorney.

She dialed the number.

"Harrington and Ferelli Divorce Attorneys," the receptionist said.

So that was it. Norm had wanted a divorce.

Myrtle smiled. "Sneaky bugger. But I beat him to it."

Yes, nothing says divorce like tea laced with rat poison and a midnight burial out in the country.

Atrophy

Aggie was stuffed.

She was so full that she couldn't digest even a single thought.

Homer stroked her hair lovingly while she stared at him, speechless. Her mouth stretched into a slight smile and he leaned forward, gently kissing her lips.

"Happy anniversary, honey. You're the love of my life, Aggie. Always have been, always will."

When a tear trickled from her eye, he wiped it away with a tissue.

"I'm not very good at this, but I want you to know that you look almost as lovely as the day we met."

* * *

In the summer of 1968, Homer Duggan's life changed forever at the Klondike Days fairgrounds in Edmonton. That was the year he had met Agnes McFadden.

Aggie.

She was in line ahead of him, her long coppery hair covered with wisps of pink cotton candy. Noticing the sticky mess, Homer reached out a scrawny hand and plucked at her hair.

"Hey!" Aggie scowled, outraged that some tall, skinny kid with freckles splayed across his nose would have the audacity to touch her.

Homer grinned. "Well, aren't you a sweet thing?"

Over the summer he followed her everywhere. He was in love. Well, as in love as any sixteen year old could be. Aggie was his dream girl, and he knew they were meant to be together…forever.

When she finally gave in and rewarded him with a date, Homer was in ecstasy. Two days later, Aggie—with hair the color of a shiny new penny and eyes as blue as the cloudless sky—became his girlfriend. A week after his nineteenth birthday he married her.

"I'll love you forever," Aggie whispered that first night.

The next morning Homer told her that he refused to have children. He loved her so much that he didn't want to share her with anyone. Aggie reluctantly agreed, and their life together was perfect.

* * *

Until last month, when Matthew Patterson moved in next door.

Homer took a steadying breath.

"It's all Patterson's fault, Aggie."

He leaned back in his chair and stared at the ceiling. Some things just had to be said, he realized. Hell, if their relationship didn't have honesty and trust, how could they possibly last?

"For better or worse, Aggie. That's what you promised. Remember?"

When she stubbornly refused to answer, he crossed his arms and glared back at her.

"If it wasn't for Matthew Patterson, none of us would be in this predicament."

Ten years younger than Homer, Patterson operated a business out of his basement. People would drop by at all hours of the day or night, carrying large packages that they left behind.

At first, Aggie and Homer suspected he was a drug dealer. Then late one night, Homer saw Patterson carrying a garbage bag out to the curb. He decided to investigate, and what he found made his stomach heave.

Immediately stomping over to Patterson's door, he pounded furiously until the man opened it.

"Homer? What are you do—"

"Explain this!" Homer growled, shoving the bag in the man's hands.

Patterson stared at it, uncomprehending. Then a slow smile crept across his face.

"What the hell's so funny?" Homer demanded.

"You must be wondering if I've slaughtered someone in here," Patterson said with a chuckle. "I can assure you, it's all quite innocent. Come inside."

Homer shuddered as he entered the pitch-black house. An unpleasant, coppery chemical smell lingered in the air. It reminded him of a hospital.

He paused at the basement door, suddenly terrified. "W-what's down there?"

"Follow me. I'll show you my masterpiece."

In the basement, Patterson flicked on a light, and Homer saw two worktables lining one wall. Over twenty glass jars were neatly labeled and stored on a nearby shelf. But it was the *thing* in the corner that made his heart skip a beat.

26

A large Doberman sat upright on the floor, its tongue lolling lifelessly to one side.

"H-he's dead!" Homer sputtered.

"Rejuvenated," Patterson corrected as he tenderly stroked the dog's shiny coat. "I'm a Pet Rejuvenator. What you found in that garbage bag came from Mrs. O'Brien's dog. Max was hit by a car yesterday."

He explained how he had preserved the dog by draining the fluids, removing its organs, then filling the body with material to maintain its shape.

Homer had to admit that the dog was mesmerizing. *Almost* lifelike. "But why?"

Patterson smiled. "I'm like GE. I bring good things to life. Mrs. O'Brien told me she'd wither away to nothing if she was left alone. She couldn't stand to be separated from Max. He was all she had left. Lots of people feel that way about their loved ones."

Homer left Patterson's house feeling slightly relieved.

When he told Aggie about their neighbor's strange business, she shrugged. "He's not doing anything illegal."

Nothing illegal, maybe. But was it right?

* * *

Homer swallowed hard.

"I should have known something was up when you started staying out late, playing *cards* with the girls."

He knew that she was going to deny it, so he shushed her. "There's no point in lying to me. Not now. I saw you go into his house."

He had confronted Patterson four days ago, knowing without a doubt that his neighbor had been messing with his wife. The man actually had the nerve to deny it, to say that it wasn't what Homer thought.

"You were sleeping with him, Aggie. And you were going to leave me for him."

Homer's throat began to burn as his anger simmered.

"Do you want him now?" he sneered, turning Aggie's head toward her lover.

Matthew Patterson's twisted atrophied body was a nightmare.

It was obscenely fastened to the basement wall with hooks and long spikes. The man's motionless eyes stared at them, unseeing. His temple was caked with crusted skin and congealed blood, and the stench of death oozed from every pore.

Almost perfect, Homer thought.

Except Patterson's stomach was deflated and he looked...*dead.*

27

"Practice makes perfect," he muttered. "I tried to remember what he showed me. I should have paid better attention when he did Max."

Of course, having a body kicking and screaming on the worktable didn't make it easy. Homer had to take a hammer to the man's head, knock him out a bit and tie him up with duct tape.

Red Green would be proud!

"I'll do a better job with you, Aggie. I promise."

He smiled at her. *A trophy bride.*

Aggie was stuffed. And almost completely drained. Tears poured from her horrified eyes and she made raspy mewing sounds that grew fainter with each dying breath. Her deceitful mouth was glued shut, but a few pieces of stuffing had escaped.

"I'll have to clip these," he murmured. "I'll glue your eyes shut too, my love. So your tears won't ruin your makeup."

Suddenly the doorbell rang.

Hurrying upstairs, Homer was greeted by a young courier who was holding a small box. Perplexed, he signed for the package and brought it inside. He opened it slowly, then wheezed in a gulp of air.

A stuffed squirrel was nestled in the bottom of the box.

A card was attached to it. It read:

My dearest Homer,

Matthew found Rocky stuck in the tree. He was dead.

I know you loved watching and feeding little Rocky so I had Matthew stuff him for you.

Happy anniversary and all my love.

Forever yours,

Aggie.

Homer sucked in a breath and struggled to slow his hammering heart.

Forever was a very long time.

Picture Perfect

When my sister, Belle, vanished back in 1956, I lost more than you could possibly imagine. And in the last fifty years, I've never told anyone what I saw. That summer day, I lost a part of my family, a piece of my heart…and I think I lost my soul as well.

* * *

In 1956, on the morning of the Calgary Summer Carnival, my baby sister and I were so giddy with excitement that our mother threatened to ground us for bad behavior. There's no worse punishment on the face of this earth than being left behind on Summer Carnival day.

Well, maybe there's one worse thing.

That morning, in the front seat of my father's pickup truck, we were crammed together like cattle at an auction. Some of the stuffing in the seat had escaped, but my father made a half-hearted attempt at fixing it by placing strips of black tape across its gaping wounds. Black tape, however, couldn't fix the broken windshield. It had rock chips in it the size of plum pits. A long spidery crack ran across the passenger side in front of me, cutting the trees and road in half. I had visions of the windshield breaking and driving sharp pieces of glass into us.

"Caroline, you have such an awful imagination," my mother scolded me when I told her my fear. "Why can't ya be more like Belle? She's not worryin'. Are ya, baby?"

Belle, in her new blue dress, patted my arm and then smiled up at our mother. "It's gonna be a perfect day."

I glared at my sister. *Traitor!*

Pouting all the way to town, I refused to even look at Belle. I plotted all the terrible things I would do to her—like make her eat candy until she puked. I'd make Belle pay. *Somehow.*

Upon reaching the Summer Carnival grounds, the truck lurched to a stop and dropped us in the middle of the parking lot. The scorching sun beamed down on us, and I swear we could have fried eggs and sausages on that road.

My father's heavy hand clamped down upon the top of my head. In his other hand, he held out three dollars.

"You watch your sister now," he said sternly. "Me an' your ma have to talk to somebody about some hay, so Belle's your responsibility. You hear me, girl?"

Belle's always my responsibility, I wanted to say. But being only eleven years old, I didn't have the courage.

So I nodded and snatched the money before he changed his mind. And then I spent the entire morning following my sister around the carnival grounds. She picked the rides we went on *and* the treats we ate. Everything was about Belle, and by lunch, I was tired of it.

Midway through the afternoon, I had a strange feeling. It felt like hungry eyes were watching us—devouring us. Every now and then, I made Belle stop walking, just so I could peer into the crowd. Faces came and went, but I saw nothing out of the ordinary. No one was paying any attention to us.

Or so I thought.

By suppertime, the feeling that we were being watched was so intense that I was sure I'd be sick. I tried to ignore the strange uneasiness tugging at the pit of my stomach. But it was impossible. I could feel a storm brewing. Yet, when I looked up at the sky, there wasn't a cloud in sight.

Belle's easy laughter caught my attention and I turned to watch her while she rode the Spinning Tops. After the ride was over, I followed her to the candy store, unable to take my gaze off her sparkling eyes and cherry-pink smile.

I had always been envious of Belle—with her long, blond, sun-kissed hair and sky-blue eyes. At five years old, my sister was the apple of my father's eye. And according to my mother, you could have made a whole pie out of her. I, on the other hand, was a *'plain Jane'*, as my father often reminded me. I was cursed with dirt-brown hair and *my* eyes were the color of ripe manure sizzling on the pavement. I'd never be the apple of anyone's eye.

When we reached the candy store, a woman behind the counter gave Belle a lollipop. I had to pay for mine, but my sister's was free.

"Because you're just so pretty and sweet," the woman told Belle. "An angel from Heaven, if I ever did see one."

She squinted at me, shook her head slowly and then looked back at Belle. I could almost hear the woman's thoughts. *That poor, plain child. How could she possibly be related to this little beauty?*

30

Barely concealing my jealousy, I pulled Belle out of the store. Outside, I plucked sticky cotton candy from her hair. Then I gave her an angry shove and watched her trip in the tall grass. When she picked herself off the ground, her brand-new dress was ripped and stained.

I almost laughed.

"Follow me," I said, heading down the wood-planked sidewalk.

I don't know why, but I felt such an irrepressible desire to hurry. Years later, I made myself believe that Destiny had called us. I told myself it was Fate—laughing and mocking me—that had thrown us like windblown corn seed into an old building at the end of the street.

Grandpa's Tymeless Fotos.

Inside the wooden framed building, brass oil lanterns cast eerie shadows on the rough pine walls. Deep burgundy and sapphire-blue curtains hung heavily on two walls, while black and white pictures lined the third. Some of the pictures were charcoal drawings. But most were somber, yellowed photographs of another time—another era. In every photograph, the women all wore fancy dresses that dragged on the ground. In the foreground of each picture, a bearded black-eyed man leaned in the doorway or against a post outside the buildings. Not one person smiled.

"Picture...*perfect*," a gravely voice said behind us.

I whipped around, startled.

An old white-haired man stepped from behind the burgundy curtain. He wore clothes like the people in the photographs and looked like no *Grandpa* I'd ever seen. He patted my sister on the head, and before I could say a word, he handed her an Orange Twist—*my* favorite candy—and Belle greedily plopped it in her mouth.

"Belle!" I protested. "We're not supposed to take anything from strangers."

Holding my head high and proud, I scowled at the old man. "Mister, you shouldn't be givin' candy to children when you don't know 'em."

His black, beady eyes twisted my heart with their intensity and turned it into ice.

I nudged Belle. "Let's get out—"

"Caroline!" the old man interrupted. "Dontcha want yer picture taken?"

I wondered for a moment how he knew my name. I was going to ask him, but Belle slipped her gooey hand into mine.

"Please, Caroline?" she begged. "A perfect day, remember?"

Sighing with resignation, I realized that we weren't leaving until my sister had her picture taken. After all, what Belle wanted, Belle always got.

31

I snuck a peek at the old man.

He nodded. Then he smiled—if you could call it a smile.

Quickly, I grabbed two dresses from a rusted metal rack. One dress was made of pink satin and lace. The other was heavy pine-green brocade. I was not surprised when Belle picked the satin dress. Closing the changing room door behind us, I slipped the brocade fabric over my head. The heavy cloth smothered me like a second skin and I itched to remove it. Instead, I pulled on a matching hat with lopsided purple plumes. Then I stared at my reflection in the mottled mirror.

If my parents could see me now.

"Look at me!" my sister pouted.

When I glanced over my shoulder, I drew in a sharp breath. Belle was a princess with her pink dress and pink hat. A pretty, angelic princess.

"You look…perfect," I said, turning back to my miserable reflection.

Scowling in the mirror, I realized just how ridiculous I looked—especially next to my baby sister. Belle was *Beauty*…while I was the *Beast*.

"We best be gettin' this over with," I muttered.

As we followed the old man, he began coughing violently. When he opened his mouth, I saw rotted gums—yellowish-black with decay—and a single gold tooth. His breath was putrid, as if something had crawled up inside of him…and died. When he rested his clawed hands on my shoulders, I flinched and a shiver of fear slithered up my spine.

Whose Grandpa was he, anyway?

The old man grinned—a devilish grin—and his gold tooth gleamed.

"You git to choose, Caroline," he said, pointing to the burgundy curtain. "Behine here, you'll git yer heart's desire. A picture worth more'n a thousand words. A perfect picture."

I nodded, unable to speak a word.

"But behine here," he continued, pointing to the blue curtain. "You'll git whatcha always git."

I was confused by his words. *What did he mean?*

"Choose!" he urged.

So, I chose my heart's desire—whatever that was.

A choking laugh erupted from deep within the old man, and the air suddenly reeked of dirty diapers and stale beer.

Suddenly I was scared—terrified I had made the wrong choice.

"Absolutely perfect," the old man whispered, opening the burgundy curtain.

A life-size photograph of Calgary, taken decades ago when the city was nothing more than a dirty cowboy town, was mounted on the wall behind the curtain. In it, a crowd of women gathered on a street corner. They all wore dresses like the ones Belle and I were wearing. The picture was so detailed that I could see jagged scars on their faces and fearful apprehension in their eyes. They seemed to be pleading with the photographer, while they avoided looking at the bearded, black-eyed man who stood stiffly in front, his arms folded across his chest and a gun gripped in one hand.

I was mesmerized by the gun.

Until the old man belched and broke the spell.

"You have a *special* place," he said, eyeing Belle and licking his cracked lips.

He positioned my sister next to the man in the photograph—the man with the gun.

Rubbing his hands together, the old man smirked. "You're up in front, Caroline."

I was stunned. It was the first time in my life that I ever stood in front of Belle—the first time that *I* was center stage.

I couldn't resist throwing a smug smile Belle's way. I kept my tongue in check, fearful that it would escape. Then I smiled boldly into the camera, and a strange surge of energy charged through my body. The flash blinded me for a moment and I was completely disoriented.

"Pick up yer picture in an hour," the old man said.

Without a word, I paid him. Then I turned to my sister. "Let's go, Belle."

A tidal wave of relief swept over me as I pushed her out the door and across the field.

"Here, Caroline," she whispered. "I snitched it for ya."

Her hand was feverishly hot as she handed me something—an Orange Twist.

I hugged her so tight that I could feel the beating of her heart and my jealousy melted into a sudden realization. *I loved my sister.* Ashamed, I leaned close to her ear to tell her just how much I loved her.

But then something terrible happened.

"Caroline?"

The fear in her voice sent shivers down my spine and I began to sense her drifting away somehow.

"Belle, I—"

"Caroline!"

Pulling away, I looked at her and gasped.

My sister was slowly disintegrating before my eyes. One moment she was solid and warm. The next, she slipped through my fingers like tiny grains of sand. Her body became transparent and I could see right through it. Her face flickered before me and her voice grew distant, barely there.

"Caroline, what's happenin' to me?"

Then my beautiful and perfect sister vanished.

Terrified, I stumbled back to *Grandpa's Tymeless Fotos* but the building was completely empty. Even the old man was gone. At first glance, the only things that remained were the burgundy curtain and the wall-sized picture. Then something caught my eye.

I slowly inched forward and retrieved a scrap of paper from the floor. It was a small photograph. A picture of me standing center stage—alone. There were no people in the background.

And no Belle.

Praying that my sister would reappear, I stared at the picture on the wall behind the burgundy curtain—the one with the women standing at the street corner.

Then I saw her.

Belle stared back at me from the wall. Her eyes pleaded with me to save her, while the man with the gun gripped her arm tightly.

Screaming until I was hoarse, I raced from that shop as if the devil himself was on my heels—the devil with one gold tooth. For a year, I couldn't speak a word out loud. It was as if my voice had vanished along with Belle.

* * *

I never told a soul about that day. Until now. I can't tell you what really happened, but I can tell you one thing—I miss my sister something fierce. Every year, I've gone back to those fairgrounds during Summer Carnival. Every year, I pray that I'll find Belle. But every time I go, there's no sign of her—or the old man from *Grandpa's Tymeless Fotos*.

Once, though, I caught sight of a young man taking pictures of children. He must have been about nineteen. When I passed by him, he gave me an evil grin.

That's when I saw it.

A familiar golden tooth.

More than a photograph was taken the day my sister disappeared. Some cultures believe a photograph steals a part of you—traps your soul forever in its picture perfect world. Some people believe the devil takes your soul.

I know they're right.

34

Sweet Dreams

I always hated camping—the strange lurking noises in the woods, the bloodsucking mosquitoes that voraciously drilled for blood...*the thin canvas of a tent that could be so easily slashed by a bear.* Then there were the shadows, pervasive and malignant, hovering in every corner. Of course, peeing in the woods wasn't my idea of a good time either.

When Justin, my husband, decided we were going on a camping trip with three other couples, I groaned and whined like an errant child. But I knew that I couldn't escape fate. So reluctantly I packed up our tents, sleeping bags and Coleman coolers stoked with more beer than food. Then we headed for the mountains and *Lac de Rêverie.*

Justin told me that meant *Lake of Dreaming.*

During the monotonous drive our newest friends, Margie and Burton, were ensnared in a deadly lip-lock. After ten minutes I avoided glancing over my shoulder and decided that they just weren't interested in the antique store we passed. Or the three elk grazing in the ditch. And Margie and Burton certainly didn't give a hoot about the dead skunk lying in the middle of the road.

For a fraction of a second I thought about interrupting their spit-swapping contest.

Instead, I slept.

* * *

It was pitch black when we arrived at *Lac de Rêverie.* Carol, my dearest friend who was already on to her third husband, Philippe, had arrived an hour ahead of us. Philippe, the *Italian Stallion* with long black hair, was busy chopping wood. I caught a glimmer of his axe illuminated by the light of five lanterns. A small fire crackled and sputtered off to one side where Carol had arranged some folding chairs.

I confiscated one and sat down.

"Wanna beer, Lexie?" Justin asked me, his new sapphire earring sparkling in the left ear.

I shook my head. I was feeling fuzzy enough without any alcohol.

"We'll be back in half an hour," Burton said with a wink. "Gonna test the temperature of the water." His grinning mouth returned to suck the air out of Margie. Strangely, she didn't seem to mind.

I suddenly pictured them skinny-dipping in the mist-shrouded lake. Yuck! So much for spending the weekend swimming!

A van lurched to a stop by our car. Dylan Hunt and his girlfriend, *Blond-Bimbo*, got out. Okay, I'll admit that's not her real name, but that's what we called her. The woman's name kept changing along with her face but Dylan, my husband's boss, always managed to find a replacement that was unbelievably dumber than the last.

"Blond-Bimbo's going to break her ankle," Carol snorted in my ear.

We stared at the woman who thought three-inch spiked heels were a trendy fashion statement in the B.C. mountains.

"Dyl, honey, can you get me some wine?" Blond-Bimbo simpered. She stumbled toward a padded chair. "I'm parched."

Dyl Honey immediately stopped setting up their tent and pulled out a bottle of wine from a cooler. He passed the woman the wine and a corkscrew, and Carol and I had to look away for fear we'd burst out laughing when the woman stared, uncomprehending, at the alien metal object. When we glanced back, Blond-Bimbo was trying to hammer the corkscrew through the metal wrapper.

Carol nudged me with her elbow. "Now isn't *she* a keeper?"

Snickering quietly, I grabbed two flashlights and whispered, *"I have to pee."*

When Carol looked at me with that *'why are you telling me'* look, I shoved a flashlight into her hand. "You're coming with me. I'm not going into these spooky old woods alone. God only knows what's lurking out there."

"Whooooooo," Carol moaned, doing an Academy Award-winning ghost impression.

It freaked the hell out of me.

Peering behind us as we followed a trail, I watched Joseph toss a log on the fire and then sit down next to Blond-Bimbo. He was laughing at something the woman had said. My fingers curled reflexively as the wildcat in me scratched to the surface.

"Oh, Lexie," my best friend said, patting my shoulder. "Don't worry about *her*. Justin isn't interested in airheads."

Swallowing hard, I realized Carol was right. Justin and I had been married for six years. Our marriage was strong.

36

Wasn't it?

"Go pee." Carol pointed to a tall cedar. Then she sat down on a wood stump.

I disappeared around the wide trunk of the tree, wedged my flashlight between some branches and squatted, praying to God that I wouldn't topple over. Although my bladder was full, I couldn't seem to relax enough to do anything.

Come on. Pee, damnit!

"So tell me more about Margie and Ben," Carol hollered after a minute.

"Burton," I corrected.

"So?" she prodded.

"Margie and Burton moved in down the road. Two months ago. They're nice enough people."

I heard Carol grunt. "Yeah, for a couple of leeches."

I laughed. "You should have been in the car for the ride up here. You wouldn't have been able to pry them apart with a crowbar. They were stuck together like Crazy Glue. I haven't seen anything like it since high school. And when they did come up for air—which was maybe once—they whispered stuff to each other like, *'you're the one, baby'* and *'it's all for you, lover'*. Oh my God! You should have been there, Carol."

"Why do men feel that they have to impress the boss?" I muttered, on a rampage. "I mean, Justin is a great employee. He works late, fills in when they call him and then invites the big boss to come *camping* with us. And he makes me find two other unfortunate couples to beg to come with us." I paused for a moment. "Sorry."

When my friend didn't answer, I realized she was probably miffed at me. I had led her to believe that the camping trip was more for the four of us—that Dylan, Blond-Bimbo, Margie and Burton were just last minute add-ons.

I stopped talking as a sudden rush of hot liquid poured onto the ground. When it veered off and began trickling down my right leg, I swore. "Oh, shit! I just peed on myself, Carol. Now I'm going to have to change my jeans. Who the hell decided to go camping anyway?" Without waiting for her answer, I snorted. "Oh, yeah. It was my darling husband."

Justin, I'm gonna kill ya!

"I mean, it was Justin's bright idea to come out here. I personally can't wait until the weekend is over. No offense, Carol. I really would have loved to have done something with just you and Philippe. You've been married for two weeks and I haven't exchanged two paragraphs with Philippe. In fact, let's make plans to do something next weekend—just the four of us."

Silence greeted me.

"What do you think?" I called out. The only response I got was the nervous chattering from invisible night birds that perched somewhere overhead.

Digging into my pocket for some tissue, I came up empty. *Some kind of camper I was!* Embarrassed, I hung my head, even though no one could see me.

"Carol? I need some toilet paper. Did you bring some?"

My best friend didn't answer me. Was she pissed off?

"Okay, this isn't funny," I whined. "I need some paper—Kleenex—anything."

Something crackled in the bushes to my left. When I turned sharply I lost my balance and one hand slid into the soil. The ground was damp and warm. Fresh pee does that.

"Shit!" Well, technically it was urine, but *shit* is what I muttered. "Carol?"

My friend was gone. She had left me stranded, alone in the heart-gripping darkness. I hastily pulled up my jeans, feeling a cold patch on the inside left thigh. Cursing under my breath, I stepped out onto the path.

Snnap!

In the dead calm of night it sounded like a gunshot, although I realized it was probably just a tree branch. I moved cautiously along the path.

Crrraack!

Abruptly, the night birds stopped twittering.

That's when I knew that something was coming for me. I could *feel* it.

A golden glimmer of light trickled through the trees and wound its way between and around the thick dense brush. As the light sinuously surrounded thick tree trunks and lush branches, every leaf and flower fell to the forest ground.

My heart pounded as the light moved closer, caressing the tree behind me. Frozen with fear, I held my breath and waited for the light to disintegrate my skin, but the eerie glow vanished as quickly as it had appeared. It was maybe fifteen minutes before I could make my legs stop trembling and force them to move forward.

Carol wasn't going to be forgiven for leaving me behind. Not for a long while. And if I ever found out that it had been Justin or one of the others out there with a flashlight…

When I reached the campsite, I stared in disbelief. The vehicles were parked by the side, the tents were pitched a few yards from the fire, and the chairs were empty. Philippe's axe glistened when my flashlight cut a path across its blade. It lay abandoned in the grass—an unusual thing for Philippe to do. Justin's beer can was jammed into the chair's cup holder. The tab hadn't even been pulled. Carol's sweater lay on the ground, trampled with dirt, moss and wine.

My stomach heaved and I struggled for air.

Everyone was gone.

"Justin?"

Nobody answered me. The only sound I heard was the oversized cooking pot boiling over. Philippe had been making stew. I peeked under the lid, partly from curiosity and partly to let the steam vent.

That's when I saw it.

At the surface of the meaty stew, a sapphire earring sparkled—still attached to Justin's ear.

"Juuuuustiiiiin!" I shrieked, feeling the air rush from my lungs. I fainted and hit the ground, hard.

* * *

I awoke abruptly as the air around me lurched to a stop.

Opening my eyes I saw that I was in the car. And Justin was driving.

"Sweet dreams?" he whispered with a smile, his earring dancing in the moonlight.

I smiled. They are now.

Relieved, I closed my eyes again. It had all been a nasty dream. My heart settled into a happy pitter-patter.

"We're here," he said a moment later.

It was pitch black but a light flickered over a sign. *Lac de Rêverie.*

Carol, my dearest friend, greeted me at the campsite. When I saw Philippe, the *Italian Stallion* with long black hair, busily chopping wood, I gasped. I caught a glimmer of his axe, illuminated by the light of five lanterns. A small fire crackled and sputtered off to one side where Carol had arranged some folding chairs.

My heart dropped into the pit of my stomach. Confused and disoriented, I confiscated a chair and sat down.

What the fu—?

"Wanna beer?" Justin asked, interrupting my thoughts.

I shook my head. I was feeling fuzzy enough without any alcohol.

"Gonna test the temperature of the water," Burton said with a wink. His grinning mouth returned to suck the air out of Margie. Strangely, she didn't seem to mind.

Philippe's eyes narrowed as he watched them, and he licked his lips. "I'll get some meat for a stew." He walked off toward *Lac de Rêverie*, the axe slicing through the air with each step.

"We'll be back in half an hour," Margie called out.

Catching a glimmer of golden light swirling around Philippe's axe, I shivered.

"To sleep, perchance to dream," I whispered, awaiting my inescapable fate...*my destiny*.

Separation Anxiety

Last night I was viciously tortured and tormented.

It began with a piercing howl that shattered the barren calm of night. When I awoke, I fervently prayed that whoever was making the godawful noise would just *shut up*.

Then I realized that it was *I* making that horrific sound.

My tormentors lurked in the shadows. I watched with eyes bulging as they approached, their droning conversation mesmerizing me. I screamed, terrified, as they descended upon me. They covered my body, their hairy fingers reaching, grasping, pinching me…

* * *

Waking abruptly from my nightmarish sleep, I struggled desperately to steady my erratic breathing. Inhaling a breath of air, I pried open my sleep-glued eyes. Confused and disoriented, I sensed that something was very, very wrong.

A void of darkness surrounded me—a heavy blanket of fear.

Every night for the past three days I have been haunted by the same harrowing nightmare. Strangers pursued me. Hundreds of them swarmed around me. I could feel them torturing my body with exquisite anguish—those faceless creatures of the night.

I hate dreaming!

I heard strangled sobs—an infant dying to be held, dying to be loved.

Struggling against the smooth coolness of satin sheets, I sighed heavily with frustration. *Will I ever get a full night's sleep?*

Nothingness enveloped me like a leather glove—slick and cool against my skin. I reached a tentative hand to my forehead. Massaging its icy surface, I could feel faint electrical impulses course along my temple. How cold I felt!

The baby's cries grew more persistent.

I must get up and feed him. Perhaps then he'll go back to sleep.

My hand groped forward, reaching for the lamp on my bedside table. Then it paused in mid-air—paralyzed. Inexplicably I yanked my hand back, frightened of touching something hideous...something other than the lamp.

"Waa!" the baby screamed.

Why doesn't Joseph go get him?

Opening my eyes cautiously, I peered into the pitch-black obscurity of night. Not even a sliver of moonlight shone through the opaque blinds of our bedroom.

How could Joseph sleep through this ruckus?

I peered into the void yet could not discern one solitary object. In fact, the room seemed devoid of anything substantial. Empty.

I must feed the baby.

Buzz...

A vaguely familiar buzzing sound interrupted my thoughts. As the irritating noise hummed closer, my hands clenched the satin sheets.

Buzzzz...

Then I heard voices, muffled and droning. I stretched tiredly, my aching muscles rebelling against the sudden movement.

Without warning, a narrow crack of light appeared along the ceiling.

A car passing by on the street outside?

My baby wailed again—his ragged sobs undulating like whitecaps on a raging sea.

I must get up.

Rolling reluctantly to one side, my forehead cracked against something unyielding.

Damn! What the hell?

I apprehensively stretched upwards, clawing at the air around me. My fingers grazed along a wall—a wall that should not be there.

When did Joseph move the bed against the wall? We've always had it in the middle of our bedroom.

Panic constricted my dehydrated throat and I edged closer to the left side, only to come up against another solid mass. A convulsive chill swept through me as I noticed that the droning buzz was just outside these walls. My fingers groped blindly above my head, encountering an unimaginable punishment—the nightmare of all nightmares. There was something peculiar above my head—a ceiling.

Oh my God! I am trapped in a box!

I blinked unblinkingly in disbelief as vague comprehension trickled through my oxygen-deprived brain and light teasingly flickered through the cracks above me. My blue-tinged lips whispered a silent plea. My ragged fingernails bit into my palms. All this, yet I felt nothing.

Suddenly, an intense light shot daggers into my eyes. I saw faces—too many to count. They were all staring sorrowfully at me, tearfully whispering my name.

"Good-bye, Maddy," their collective voices murmur.

Good-bye? Am I going somewhere?

Then my husband's face appeared. He raised one hand and lashed out at something in the air.

Joseph? What's going on?

He ignored me. Darling, irritating Joseph was sobbing.

There's no reason to cry, Joseph, my love.

My gaze traveled across the strange box that encompassed me and I realized that I was dead wrong. There was a reason to cry…and scream.

I was in a coffin.

Is this some practical joke? I'm not dead.

"Goodbye, Maddy," Joseph moaned.

Listen to me, Joseph. I'M NOT DEAD!

"At least now you'll be with our son," Joseph whispered in my ear.

Our son?

He caressed my frigid cheek, leaned down and kissed my lips.

Wait, Joseph! What happened to the baby?

Somewhere a wailing baby drifted into oblivion.

Then I remembered…

Our baby was dead!

* * *

I remembered finding his unconscious body in the crib. He had reacted violently to a single bee sting. It had triggered a deadly allergic reaction with the devastating force of a nuclear weapon. His tiny, frail body could not defend itself against the lethal invasion. The bee's poison had attacked each cell, replicating its infection and swarming into his lungs.

Sobbing and wailing incessantly, I had rocked him in my arms, watching helplessly as my poor baby's head swelled grotesquely. Ten minutes before the paramedics arrived, his respiration had ceased with a final droning hiss of breath. My beloved baby who had only breathed our polluted air for three days had died from the bee's venom.

I always believed that payback was the sweetest form of revenge.

Mad with grief, I hunted down the buzzing sound that dared me to destroy its malignancy. Its owner—a plump Queen bee. I chased that *bee-atch* all over the house with a fly swatter. Yet, she escaped, laughing and droning triumphantly.

"Go ahead, you murderous bitch. Make my day!" I had screamed at her.

Cackling hysterically, I finally crushed that stupid bitch, her guts splattering all over my kitchen window. One minute she had been buzzing defiantly—the next, I had silenced her forever.

Then a weird thing happened.

While I was cleaning her remains from the glass, I noticed another bee outside. It hovered furtively, witnessing every move I made. I knew then that it was one of the Queen's loyal workers. A shiver of trepidation slithered up my back as I locked eyes with that bee. Then it flew off and I released a titanic sigh of relief.

* * *

A sympathetic voice jostled me back to the present, followed closely by the sibilant sound of doom.

"I'll miss you, Madeleine," my mother wept, choking on my name. Her lips kissed my cosmetic-coated face. "What a terrible way to die."

"Yes," Joseph agreed, his handsome face wavering before me.

Then he shook his head in disbelief. "It was horrifying. Who would ever have thought that a swarm of bees would attack a human being like that? Maddy was completely covered—only her eyes were left untouched. It was almost as if they wanted her to watch, to see what they were doing to her."

Oh God!

Memories of burning pain sliced through my mind. I remembered the heat of their bodies engulfing me in a jacket of gold and black fuzz. I had staggered with arms flailing, trying to dislodge the ungodly hoard attached to my already bloating body. I could still hear their deafening roar. It was like standing at the edge of a railroad while a locomotive endlessly whizzed by.

"The bastards!" Joseph muttered. "I'd like to kill the whole bloody hive."

"At least Maddy is not suffering anymore," my mother rasped.

I screamed silently as Joseph's hand caressed the coffin lid. Panic gripped my mindless body and my stomach rebelled, churning bloodlessly. I fought against a tide of nausea, although my body was physically empty.

But I'm still alive! Aren't I? How could I see or hear any of you if I wasn't?

Comprehension dawned and I realized that my soul still lingered. Too many things had been left undone—unsaid. I could no longer move anything but my soul's eyes. I was hearing through my soul's ears.

But I, Madeleine Anne Decker, was dead.

What the hell is that godawful noise?

BUZZ...

* * *

I gasped airlessly when a diminishing ray of light grazed across a sinister specter.

The worker bee was inside my coffin—its feathery legs whispering closer to my face.

Get it out! Don't close the lid!

I cursed my motionless lips.

As the coffin lid firmly closed, I was trapped with the endless buzzing of vengeance. I could feel the bee's microscopic legs tickling my cheek, tormenting me as he made his way furtively across my face. When he reached my nose, his droning hum vibrated forcefully, shattering the cartilage under my skin.

I sensed his thoughts, his desire for revenge...for justice. I had irreverently murdered his Queen—his mother. I had, in essence, ripped her asunder and torn her from *her* family. And he had returned the favor.

The coffin rocked slightly.

I was being lowered into the decaying, musty earth, and soon I heard the muffled sound of dirt being packed on top, surrounding and severing me from all that I loved...separating me from Life.

Separation from those you love is torture. There is no worse torment than to be ripped apart from those you hold most dear. It is a terror of the soul. Nothing can compare to the pounding of your heart, extreme breathlessness and the endless aching that you feel.

BUZZZZ...

The worker bee flew into my left nostril and Death swarmed into my icy corpse, claiming my unrepentant soul for all eternity.

I should have asked for the strength to forgive and for forgiveness for my own sin. I realized that now. Instead, I hungered for revenge and feasted on the annihilation of a Queen. Together, we had created a vicious circle of death, and all because I had thirsted for *payback*.

I had always believed that payback was the sweetest form of revenge.

I realize now...I was wrong—dead wrong.

Payback can also *bee*...murder!

45

The Car

I'm looking scary right now, with my leftover eye-makeup smeared under my eyes. The seams of the saggy bags under them betray my lack of sleep. I didn't get to *slip away* into a peaceful sleep like the rest of you probably did last night. Instead I got to call 911.

Twice.

And before you freak out and wonder who had a heart attack, it wasn't like that. *Well...not really.*

It all started when Royale, the most wonderful guard dog of all, began barking at two this morning and wouldn't shut up. So Marc, my hero, went to see why. He told me later he had heard voices. Not *that* kind of voices...*real* ones! He looked out our side windows, then the front ones. Royale, our fluffy white miniature American Eskimo *killer watchdog*, continued barking and growling.

Then Marc saw someone run across the street, stop in the middle, look both ways then run back towards our house. That's when he saw the shadows hiding behind the neighbor's gate.

By this time I was thinking that my hero needed backup, so I crawled out of bed and went to see what he was doing. I was shocked when he told me there were kids outside. I looked out the window and saw them huddling by the gate. Six—count 'em—*six* teens, probably no more than fifteen years old, were wandering the streets of Edmonton at 2:00 a.m. They were hiding in my neighbor's back yard.

Marc started yelling at them. "Hey! What are you doing?" When they didn't answer, he shouted, "Get out!"

One of the kids—a boy, I think—shouted something back. "Someone's after us." Some of the kids snickered.

"Get out or I'm going to call the cops!" Marc yelled.

Of course, me being proactive and all, I made my first ever 911 call. I explained to the cops that there were six young teens hiding in my

46

neighbor's yard. I also told them that they said someone was after them, but that it was impossible to determine whether they were seriously scared or not. As Marc put it, why wouldn't they bang on doors if they felt threatened?

The kids, seeing me in the window talking to someone on the phone, quickly banded together and ran across the street. They hovered in the path to Sobeys for a moment, then disappeared.

I have to admit, the entire thing left me feeling a bit unnerved. What if the kids were in *real* danger? What if someone 'bad' was after them? What if they had just vandalized my neighbor's yard or house? What if it was local drug deal gone bad and the dealers were hunting them down? What if they were all running away? What if they came back? What if I had imagined it all and they never really existed?

What if...?

Sometimes being a fiction writer with a vivid imagination is exhausting!

Marc and I had to wait, of course. We stood in the dark near the windows, but not too close in case someone decided to drive by and shoot the witnesses. I waited for the gunshots.

And then we saw it.

The car.

One lone car cruising ever so slowly down our quiet little street.

We ducked behind the blinds. Did the driver see us? Did he have a shotgun in the passenger seat? Maybe we just imagined that the car had anything to do with those kids. *Group hysteria with only two people? Is that possible?*

A car motor chugged. And then the same car slinked past our window...*again.*

"Call the cops, Cheryl," Marc said quietly.

Do you get charged extra when you actually *use* 911? I made two calls last night and I'm sure they're going to bill me.

"Ah, yeah, I called about five minutes ago," I said to the dispatcher. "I reported a gang of six teens in my neighbor's back yard. Well, there's a strange car that has—Wait! There it is again!"

The car slowed, its interior dark and eerie as it passed in front of my house. It drew parallel with my window.

And then it idled.

I couldn't breathe. It felt like the air from the room had been instantly sucked out.

A cop's voice asked me for a description. When he asked if I could see the license plate number, I wanted to smack the officer through the phone. I'm standing in my pajamas in my living room/Marc's office, looking out a window into the dark of night. How the hell would I see the plate number?

"It's a silver T-bird," Marc said, moving closer to the window.

I relayed the information to the dispatcher who said they'd have a car sent over right away. When I hung up, Marc shook his head in disbelief. "They actually thought we could see the license plate?"

I snorted in disdain. "Yeah. I wanted to say, 'Wait, I'll get out my laser-scoped sniper rifle and check.'"

Marc chuckled and sat down in his office chair.

"We have binoculars," I said. "Somewhere." I had won a pair a few years ago and even used them at a concert. *Once.* I haven't seen the binoculars since.

We saw the car pull away from our curb and continue slowly down the road. A minute later it turned around and rolled past again.

"The car," I said to Marc who had moved away from the window. "It's back."

We watched as the *phantom*-car patrolled the street, back and forth. Suddenly it stopped.

A man with a husky build climbed out. He looked around and I am sure he stared right at us. Could he see us watching him in the dark from our window? His eyes scoped out the shadows between the houses. He cupped both hands to his mouth and yelled something but we couldn't make out the words.

Was he just a terrified father looking for his kids? Or someone who wanted to hurt them?

By this time, Marc had dug out the pair of binoculars from the mysterious *'somewhere'*. He probably got them from the same place that ate our socks—or at least one of each pair. Of course binoculars would have solved the license plate mystery. But that would have made too much sense, and neither of us was thinking clearly. Hell, we had been in a dead sleep half an hour earlier.

Another ten minutes went by. There was no sign of the teens, but that damned car kept creeping along our street. We could see the parking lot of the Sobeys too. What the heck was going on there? Cars...lots of cars.

And then a police car went by the Sobeys, with its lights flashing. Relief set in. The police took a while but it looked like they were finally on the job. *Whew!*

The shrill ringing of our phone startled us, cutting through the quiet darkness of our unlit house.

"We're on our way," a cop said.

Confused, I said, "But wasn't that you in front of Sobeys with your lights flashing?"

"No, we just turned off onto 34th," came the reply. They were still three minutes away.

What the hell was going on out there?

I reminded the officer about the silver Thunderbird that kept slowing down by our house and he assured me they'd check it out. Ten minutes later, a police car drove past our house. It had been about forty minutes since Marc had first discovered the kids hiding in my neighbor's yard.

And of course me being a good neighbor and all, I had to phone them—after two in the morning—to let them know that, once again, they were sleeping through all the exciting action that our quiet street gets every third year. Darrel and Debbie's lights flicked on, front and back. Great, now we weren't the only ones awake.

I glanced at Marc who was peering through the tiny concert binoculars. "Don't let anyone see you using those," I warned. "They'll think you're a Peeping Tom."

"I need night vision goggles," Marc said seriously. Maybe a little *too* seriously.

He's been watching too many Bruce Willis and Arnie movies lately. But Marc is ex-military too. You know, trained to kill with a single deadly pinch or cosmic stare. Although if you saw my *licensed-to-kill hero* dressed in his faded, ratty blue housecoat, carrying a miniscule pair of 'noculars in one hand, the other frantically trying to keep the tie on his housecoat from coming undone...

The cars in the Sobeys' lot started to separate and a black sports car zoomed past our house.

"It has nothing to do with this," Marc said confidently.

The same black sports car zoomed past again, and I had a sudden thought. What if the silver car could change colors? Change styles? Reality set in. What if another gang was after these kids? What if...?

"Go to bed," Marc groaned when I voiced my thoughts.

Instead I dragged the chair from *my* office, sat beside him and watched the window like it was opening night for the next blockbuster. All I needed was the buttered popcorn. After a few minutes of inactivity, our window view became boring. Tiredness set in. There was nothing more we could do. So we did what we do best.

We went back to sleep.

I tossed and turned for about ten minutes. What *were* those kids up to? Were they in danger? Were their parents looking for them? Was that what all the cars were about? And if not, then how come those parents had no idea that their kids were cruising the streets and getting into trouble?

Just as I was fading off to sleep, I prayed that the kids would be all right. And I cursed the parents who probably slept mindlessly while *I* worried about *their* children.

In the final moment of consciousness, I heard one final sound before slipping into an exhausted sleep.

A dull chugging that sent shivers up my spine.

The car...

Deadly Reunion

I was just sitting down at my desk with a mug of nuked coffee and a week-old whole wheat bagel when the email arrived—the one that changed my life forever.

The subject line read: *I knew you in high school* :-)

The happy face suggested the sender was happy to reconnect.

I glanced at the sender's name. *Amanda Decker.*

I didn't recall going to school with anyone by that name, but I opened the email anyway.

Hi JoLynne, this is Amanda Williams Decker. Remember me?

Nope.

I found your email addy on your website, which I came across when I was looking for some books to download.

An ebook lover. Well, that deserved a brownie point or two.

We were in grade eleven and twelve together. I hung around with Georgia Burns and Mallory Finklestein.

Who?

You and I had a crush on the same guy. Jackson Pierce.

Ah...I did remember *him*. How could anyone forget the legendary Jackson Pierce, captain of the football team? He was God's gift to hormonal teenage girls back then. The perfect excuse for daydreaming in class. Or for going on one diet after the other.

I still didn't remember Amanda Williams Decker.

Until I read the next line.

I'm the one who caught you and Jackson behind the bleachers after the provincial championships.

It all came flooding back. That final game when the whole school erupted. The screaming of fans during half-time. The thundering of the drums and blaring of the trumpets as the school band mangled traditional band songs. The stomping of feet and clanging of metal bleachers.

And my very first kiss.

Jackson had sent a note via a chain of willing hands. He'd invited me to celebrate his half-time success by meeting him under the bleachers for *something special*. Naively, I'd thought he meant a drink, something he'd snuck in when the coach wasn't looking. I was all for a quick sip of something tantalizing and illegal.

But Jackson had something else on his mind.

"Hey," he said when I ducked under the bleachers. "Over here."

He was alone. Tall, muscular, golden-haired, blue-eyed. Ah…

"I got your note," I said, trying to sound calm.

I wanted him to think it didn't matter if he'd asked me or not. Like all the other girls in the school, I was hopelessly in love with Jackson. Or I thought I was. He never noticed me though—until a week earlier, in Language Arts. He was having problems understanding the complexities of grammar construction, something for which I had a natural talent.

Ignoring the clamor above us, I stared up into those deep blue eyes and was lost for a moment, somewhere between earth and heaven.

"Something wrong?" he asked, frowning.

I came crashing back to earth. "No." I cleared my throat. It felt like I'd swallowed a mouthful of dust bunnies, complete with tails. "You said you had something special?"

Jackson smiled. I swear I heard a *ca-ching* sound, his smile was so golden.

"I do," he said. "And it's just for you."

"What is it? Did you sneak in some beer?"

He shook his head.

"Not cigarettes," I said, my eyes widening with horror. "We'll set off the smoke detectors."

Jackson chuckled. "You don't smoke."

My heart fluttered. Oh my God. The cutest guy in school knows I don't smoke. What else did he know about me?

"I have a tradition," he said, moving slowly toward me. "Call it a game tradition. Have you heard of it?"

"No."

He took my hands in his. "This tradition has helped me win every important game, and tonight is extra special because there's a scout in the bleachers somewhere."

"That's so awesome," I said, trying not to think of the heat that passed between his hands and mine. It was impossible.

"I need you to help me continue my tradition."

I nodded excitedly. "Of course, I'll help you. Whatever you need, just ask."

Jackson's smile beamed even wider. "You're a real sport."

Sport? That didn't sound very romantic.

He cupped my face, his fingers feathery light against my cheeks.

I couldn't breathe.

When he leaned down, his eyes half-closed, it hit me. Oh my God! Jackson was going to kiss me. Right there. Right then. My first kiss.

I felt his breath, warm and minty fresh, tease my delicate skin. He stopped, barely an inch from my mouth. I leaned into him, but he turned his face, his mouth brushing against my cheek, his breath quickening.

"Not yet," he whispered. "Not quite yet."

His hands slid from my face, down my shoulders and arms.

"Jackson…"

"Trust me."

And stupidly, I did.

When his hands grazed the front of my t-shirt, I sucked in a startled breath. Sensations sparked in an area where no boy had gone before. As my best friend would have said, the headlights turned on and the engine revved.

Jackson's engines were revving too.

"All I need is one feel," he said softly, persuasively.

"What do you mean?"

"You're my good luck charm." He pinned me against the back wall and slid his hands beneath my shirt. "One feel and I'll win the game."

Icy reality slapped me across the face. "This is your surprise? You want to feel me up, then finish the game?"

Before I could say another word, footsteps approached.

"Jackson, you in there?" A female voice.

I was afraid to move. Afraid she'd see me standing there, with Jackson's hands on my skin.

"Don't make a single sound," Jackson hissed in my ear.

I peered over his arm. A shadow moved toward us, female in form but unrecognizable other than having long hair.

"There you are," the girl said, sounding relieved.

"Get lost, Mandy," Jackson snarled.

"What are you doing over—"

I could feel the heat from her fiery gaze and I swear I could almost smell her anger. It was like a combination of diesel and nervous sweat.

"You brought another girl here?" Mandy squealed.

"Be quiet!" Jackson said, releasing me.

"But I'm your good luck charm," the girl said. "That's what you said at the last game. When you won. Remember? You won because of me."

"We won because I'm damned good."

I stepped to one side, uneasy about the increasing fury I heard in Jackson's voice. "Maybe we should—"

"What?" Jackson snapped. "You want us to lose?"

Mandy moved into what light there was under the bleachers. She was a chubby girl, maybe twenty pounds overweight with bad acne. She wore all black. Black jeans, black shirt, black eyes and lips.

Emo Girl. That's what we called her behind her back.

What had Jackson seen in her?

"If we lose," Jackson said, gritting his teeth, "it'll be *your* fault, Joanne."

"JoLynne," I corrected.

He shrugged. "Whatever."

That's when I realized just what a perv Jackson was. All the pieces of the puzzle slipped neatly into place, and I finally *got* it. Jackson was a narcissistic user. He went after the naïve unpopular girls to prove he could. He targeted the easy prey—emos like Mandy, geeks like me. Virgins.

Mandy's gaze drifted back to me. I wanted more than anything to meld into the faux wood panels, become one with the drywall behind them.

"You're that Birmingham girl," Mandy said.

Damn! Last thing I wanted was for her to recognize me. I'd be the talk of the school now. The buzz of the bitches. Hot news traveled fast in Westmont High.

I crossed my arms protectively. "It doesn't matter who I am."

During our little exchange, neither of us noticed that Jackson, school hero that he was, had inched toward the exit. I yearned for him to take me away. But that wasn't going to happen. Without a word, he disappeared and I was alone with Mandy Williams.

I looked at her. She was rubbing her forehead with one hand, eyes squinting as if she had the mother of all migraines. Maybe she did. She didn't look too good.

I rubbed my sweaty palms against my jeans, praying she wouldn't notice how scared I was. Then I plastered a tight smile on my face. "Jesus, what an idiot I am."

"A dead idiot," Mandy said.

"What did you say?"

I felt her eyes piercing mine and I shivered.

"I said you're a dead girl."

Her words haunted me day and night. I became paranoid. I saw Mandy in every shadowed corner and behind every bush. I heard her voice even when no one else was around.

Was I scared of her? Damn right I was.

During the last weeks of school and all through prom, I kept my eye out for Mandy Williams. Every time I saw her, she'd scowl at me, spin on one heel and storm away, a whirlwind of emotional angst in her trail.

And now Mandy was reaching out. Four years later.

Why?

The last line of her email read: *I'll be coming to Edmonton for a business meeting this Wednesday and I'd love to get together, maybe have lunch. What do you say?*

I'd say she was freaking nuts. We never hung around in high school. So why would we do that now?

Because I was curious.

There was no denying that my inquiring mind wanted to know what Emo Girl had been up to the past four years. Part of me wanted to let her know I wasn't that geeky girl in high school anymore. I was a writer.

Okay, well I wasn't *as* geeky.

Before I could weigh the consequences, I fired off an email inviting Mandy to lunch at Chez Cora. Then I logged off and went back to work on the young adult novel I was writing.

* * *

Chez Cora was busy as usual and I was seated at a table in the middle. I was about fifteen minutes early and had already tucked into a glass of house wine. I glanced around the room, taking in the mix of business and casual patrons.

My gaze clashed with a familiar set of eyes. Julie Bell, from the newspaper I often wrote articles for, was having lunch with a man I didn't recognize. He wore sunglasses and had a neatly trimmed moustache and goatee. Kind of the tall, dark and mysterious type. Julie reached out a hand, laughed at something he said and the man grabbed her hand and kissed it.

Love was in the air.

I sure hoped Julie's husband didn't catch her. I'd met Ed Bell at a Christmas party. He was the exact opposite of tall, dark and mysterious.

"JoLynne!"

My head jerked in the direction of the voice. I was stunned.

As Mandy approached, I took in her sleek appearance and confident smile. Gone was the jet black hair. She was a rich brunette now, with chin-length hair cut into voluminous layers. Gone were the heavy black eyes. Her makeup was light, expertly applied and natural looking. Gloss highlighted her lips and there was a sparkle of happiness in her blue eyes.

"M-Mandy," I stammered, rising to my feet.

"It's so great to see you after all these years." She gathered me in her arms and hugged me—like we were the best of friends.

"You too." I hugged her quickly, then stepped back, self-conscious of the looks we were getting.

Mandy sat down and took a minute to arrange the cloth napkin over her skirt. "I'm glad you had time to take a break from your busy schedule and meet me for lunch."

"I almost couldn't take the time off."

I don't know why I felt the necessity to lie, but I did.

The waiter arrived and Mandy order a glass of red wine.

"What's good here?" she asked, flipping through the menu.

"Everything."

"What are you having?"

"The chicken salad."

"That sounds good." She closed the menu.

We ordered and minutes later our salads arrived. Mandy gave me a nod, as though I'd made the right selection and she was surprised. While munching on crisp greens, we chatted about high school, rehashing some of the highlights of prom year. Most sentences started with "Remember when…?"

She seemed to know a lot about me. What classes I'd taken. My friends. She never once mentioned Jackson.

"So what do you remember about me?" she asked, grinning.

Truthfully, I didn't remember much about Mandy Williams. Other than that one time under the bleachers. I sure as hell wasn't going to remind her about that.

"I remember that you were pretty shy back then. And you liked black."

Mandy chuckled. "Yeah, good old Emo Girl."

My brow arched. "Emo Girl?"

"Come on, JoLynne. Did you really think I didn't know what kids were calling me behind my back?" There was a trace of hurt in her eyes. "I heard the snickers, the names."

"Sorry."

Mandy shrugged. "It's okay. It's all in the past."

"You seem to be doing well," I said, hoping it was true.

"I am. I'm married to a great man and my career is going very well."

"What do you do?"

"I'm an ad exec. For a major sports team."

My mind drifted a bit at the mention of sports. I didn't even follow the Oilers. My idea of a sports event was spending a couple of hours

56

alone at my computer with a pitcher of margarita mix, while playing World of Warcraft online with complete strangers.

"And you're an author," Mandy said, as if I had the most fascinating career of all.

"Yeah. Writing has always been my…thing."

"I remember that about you."

Half an hour later, I was feeling more at ease. We'd discussed our careers, her husband and my lack of a boyfriend. I was on a break, I'd told her, though break from what, I hadn't a clue. It had been six months since I'd gone out on a date, and that had ended miserably.

"So you're just in town for the day?" I asked, pushing my empty plate aside.

She shook her head. "Actually, I have no idea when I'll be leaving. My boss wants me to handle some potential clients and secure a new deal that's in the works." She gave me a wry look. "Not quite what I expected."

"Where are you staying?"

"Sawridge Inn."

My eyes widened. "Really? That's just down the road."

"I know. I couldn't believe it when you told me where this restaurant was."

"The house I'm renting is only a ten minute drive from here."

Mandy laughed. "What are the chances?"

I watched her and wondered the same thing.

* * *

That night, I thought about Mandy. She seemed to have really gotten her life together, and as I looked around the small house I was renting, I wondered where mine had gone. Sure, I loved writing. But truth be told, I didn't make much money on my novels.

The real money came from writing magazine and newspaper articles, and I just wasn't enjoying them as much. My last story had been on a Ponzi scheme that had swept through the city. A province-wide warrant was issued for Matthew Bixby, the man who'd started it. My story had been an exposé on Bixby, on how he'd swindled people in Florida, duping them out of hundreds of thousands of dollars before jumping the border. The case gave me my first cover story.

"You're a wordsmith," I said to my reflection in the bathroom mirror.

A happy tune sang out from my computer. I had an email.

Sinking into the chair, I made a silent bet it was from Mandy. She probably wanted to do dinner since she was in town for a while. We'd parted ways outside Chez Cora's with the hint of possible future plans.

I opened my email program. A single email was in the Inbox. From 20vengeanceissweet06@hotmail.com.

Who the hell was that?

Thinking it was spam, I was about to delete it when I noticed my name in the preview screen. Spammers didn't usually personalize their emails.

JoLynne, your time has come.

That was it. No signature. Nothing else but that one sentence.

"My time for what?" I muttered, trying to ignore the unease that ate at my stomach. "Am I the winner of a lottery? Am I going to meet the man of my dreams?"

All joking aside, this email didn't have a ring of humor to it.

"*Your* time has come," I said to the email.

I clicked and sent it to the trash.

Something clanged just below my bedroom window.

Damned neighbor's cat probably got into the garbage again.

I went downstairs, thoughts of getting a cat trap on my mind. I headed for the back door and was about to unlock it when a shadow streaked past the window in the door. A large shadow. Human sized.

My hand froze inches from the deadbolt. "Who's there?"

Silence.

I waited a moment, then pressed my face against the glass. "Hello? Anybody out there?"

Nothing moved.

I hadn't realized I was holding my breath until it came out in a rush. I stepped away from the door. I was about to turn away when I glimpsed the shadow again. It was moving toward the door.

"I called the police," I yelled, hoping the fear in my voice didn't betray my lie. "They're on their way."

A blurred face pressed up against the door window.

I screamed.

The face stared at me with voluminous eyes that didn't seem human.

A mask, I realized. He was wearing a mask.

I reached for the phone and called 911.

By the time I'd connected, the face was gone.

The dispatcher sent a patrol car by anyway.

"The intruder might still be around," the woman said, "so keep your doors and windows locked."

Yeah, like I was going to unlock them now.

Five minutes passed and there was a knock at the door. I saw the whirring lights of the cruiser parked in front, but I still asked the detective to hold his badge up to the window.

When I opened the door, he smiled slightly. "You reported a disturbance?" He was a bulky fellow with a roll across his stomach and a scar on his right cheek.

"Someone had their face right up to this window," I said, trying not to stare at his scar.

After a quick inspection of the yard and house, the detective said, "Looks like he's gone, ma'am. Has this happened before?"

I shook my head.

"Have you had any strange phone calls, maybe hang-ups?"

"No."

"What about mail? You get any weird packages?"

I shook my head again. Then I recalled the email.

"I guess this could be taken a number of ways," the detective said after reading the email. "I'll make a note of the header info and have one of our techs check out the account it was sent from, see if we can identify the sender."

"What should I do now?"

He sighed and shifted his belt, one hand resting lightly on the revolver tucked into it. "Not much you can do. At least not unless he contacts you again."

"I don't want him to contact me again."

He gave me a sympathetic nod. "Keep your doors and windows locked at all times." He glanced around. "You might want to get a security system. Or a dog. I'll have another car come by tonight. Maybe a couple of times. Sometimes a police presence can keep shady people away."

When he was gone, I felt tiny shivers run up my back and arms. Everywhere I looked I thought I'd see a masked intruder. I didn't want to go into another room. I turned on all the lights and put the TV on low. I got up every twenty minutes and checked the locks—just in case I missed one.

Then I sat in my mother's rocking chair, the one she'd inherited from her grandmother. Mom had given it to me last year when she was "cleaning house". Rocking almost obsessively, I thought about the face with the huge staring eyes.

There was no way I was going to sleep tonight.

My computer dinged. I had mail.

Clasping my sweater together with a fist, I approached my computer, wishing I could ignore it or turn it off. But I couldn't.

I read the email and swallowed hard.

You haven't changed a bit. BITCH.

Should I call 911 again?

After a minute of pondering, I decided to wait. If the detective traced the first message, the case would be solved. The email address of the sender for the second message was the same.

Should I reply? Well, no one had told me not to.

I sat down and typed up a four word response. *What do you want?*

The reply came within a minute. *I want you to pay.*

Pay for what?

For your transgressions.

What transgressions?

Your conceit.

Why are you doing this?

Two minutes passed.

I tried again. *What have I done to you?*

Five minutes passed. Then ten. Whoever he was, he was gone.

I stared at the screen, almost willing more words to appear, but nothing moved. Another ten minutes and I gave up.

I went back to my rocking.

* * *

Just after eight the following morning, the phone rang. It was Mandy.

"Sorry it's so early," she said.

"That's okay. I was up anyway."

"Are you free for breakfast, JoLynne?"

"I don't know…" I thought of the intruder. Could it have been Mandy? And if so, what the hell did she want?

There was only one way to find out.

"Yeah," I said. "Where do you want to meet?"

"How about my hotel? I hear they put on a great spread."

After a quick shower, I dried my hair and swept it up into a ponytail. Then I used concealer to cover the dark circles beneath my eyes and added a dab of lip gloss and a brush of blush.

I stared in the mirror. Who was I trying to impress, anyway?

On the way to Mandy's hotel, I noticed a black sedan two cars behind me. It took every road I did. The windshield was tinted, which was illegal in Edmonton, and I couldn't make out the driver, but I was positive he was following me.

I shivered. "Okay, buddy, let's see if I'm imagining things."

At the last possible moment, I took an off-ramp. I heard a screech of tires behind me as the driver of the sedan swerved to make the detour. Now he was directly behind me. And definitely following me. Shaking, I kept my speed up, driving away from the safety of Mandy's restaurant.

60

The sedan crept closer and I shrieked when its front bumper grazed my car. I spotted my salvation. A police station two blocks away. I zigged into the right lane without signaling. I wrenched the steering wheel and my car squealed into the parking lot. The black sedan sped past me. I stared after it until it disappeared, another ant lost in the streaming mob of morning rush hour.

I blew out a relieved breath and glanced at the doors to the police station. I could report the sedan, but I didn't have much proof. Besides, the driver could argue he was heading in the same direction. And no harm was done.

I climbed out and examined the bumper. A faint scrape, that was it.

With a sigh, I settled into the driver's seat, shifted the car into drive and headed back to Mandy's hotel. When I arrived I was nearly ten minutes late.

"Sorry," I said when I approached the table.

"I was going to call you," Mandy replied, "but I didn't have your cell number. Everything all right?"

"Yeah, just had to take a detour."

Mandy's eyes narrowed. "You look tired, JoLynne."

"I didn't get much sleep last night." Correction, I didn't get *any* sleep, but I was going to tell her this.

Mandy chewed her bottom lip for a moment. "Is something wrong?"

I stared at her, wondering what kind of car she drove. "What do you mean?"

"You look...I don't know. Maybe I'm imagining things, but you look worried." She paused. "I know we weren't the best of friends in school, but I am a good listener you know, so if something's bothering you—"

"Nothing's bothering me, Mandy." My tone was much sharper than I'd intended. I frowned, then let out a sigh. "Someone was messing around outside my house last night."

"Oh my God. Did they break in? Are you hurt?"

Mandy sounded sincere, but there was something odd in her expression. Her eyes didn't meet mine, not completely.

The waiter came by and took our orders, giving me a few minutes to compose myself. When the waiter left, I took a sip of water and said, "I've also been getting weird emails."

"From who?"

I shrugged. "I don't know."

Mandy opened her mouth as if she were about to say something, then clamped her lips tight.

61

"Seems kind of weird that these emails started right when you come to town," I said.

"What are you implying?"

"I'm not implying anything, Mandy. Just saying."

Our meals arrived and we dug into them wordlessly. After a few minutes, Mandy raised her eyes. "JoLynne, you'd better be really careful the next couple of days."

I gaped at her. "Is that a threat?"

"No," she said, her cheeks reddening. "I just think that since you're getting weird emails and someone was traipsing about in your yard, you should be careful. There are a lot of nutcases out there."

I wondered if she was one of them.

Mandy paid for breakfast.

"My treat," she said, before walking me outside to the parking lot.

"Do you have a vehicle?" I asked.

She nodded. "A rental. Why?"

"I thought you might like to come for dinner before you left."

It was a lie. I really wanted to know what kind of car she drove.

Mandy smiled. "That would be nice."

"How about tonight?"

"Works for me. What time?"

"Seven o'clock? I tend to eat late on the weekend."

"Perfect. I'll see you then."

I watched as she vanished inside the hotel. With a brief glance around the lot, I determined there were two dark sedans that looked similar to the one that had terrorized me. No one else was in the area so I strolled over to one of the sedans. It was black, but no tinted windshield. The other one was a dud too.

* * *

I usually don't write on Saturdays. It's the one day I allow myself to dwell on the novel I'm writing, to ferment the plot, so to speak. This Saturday, the only plotting going on was my imagination.

I spent most of the day looking out various windows and checking for mysterious sedans. I didn't see anything out of the ordinary except dark clouds gathering in the east. A storm was on its way.

I checked my email every ten minutes. No weird emails either.

Finally, I stretched out on the couch and settled into some reading. Lancelot's Lady, a romantic suspense, had been waiting far too long for my attention. Besides, I needed to find out who was after the main character Rhianna and whether the handsome but brooding Jonathan would save her.

I tried to ignore the flapping sound that came from outside my front door. One of the numbers on my house was loose and I'd been planning to screw it down, but hadn't gotten around to it yet.

Flap, flap.

The wind picked up speed, howling through the stove vent.

In the kitchen, a pot of spaghetti sauce simmered on the stove and I inhaled the delicious scent. I wasn't a gourmet cook, but I made a wicked pasta sauce. A roll of garlic bread and a Caesar salad would finish off the meal. For dessert I'd picked up a lemon cheesecake, one of my weaknesses, as evidenced by my cellulite thighs.

Rain poured in torrents, then eased up to a slight pitter-patter.

A thought crossed my mind. The flapping had stopped. Thank God.

Reading didn't prove to be as enjoyable as I'd hoped. Every time a car backfired outside, I jumped from the couch, holding my Kobo ereader in front of me as though it were a deadly weapon.

By six-thirty that evening, the rain had stopped and the sun had put in an appearance. When the doorbell rang, I blew out a sigh of relief.

Hurrying to the door, I opened it. "Mandy, I sure hope you like spag—" I choked back a scream when I saw the mutilated remains of my neighbor's cat.

A car pulled up along the curb and Mandy stepped out. She smiled and waved, while I stared at her in horror. A second later, my mind registered the fact that she was driving a blue Mazda, not a black sedan.

She approached my house, a bottle of wine in her hand. "I hope white wine is okay."

"Stop!" I said.

"What's wrong?"

"Someone killed my neighbor's cat and left it…" I pointed to the porch.

"Jesus! Are you okay?" Mandy rushed forward and ushered me inside. "Sit down on the couch."

"I think I should call the police."

"Did you see who did it?"

I shook my head. "The doorbell rang. I thought it was you."

"I just got here. You don't really think I did this, do you?"

My hands were shaking so hard I tucked them between my knees. "I don't know what to think. First I get weird emails. Then someone's in my yard, staring into my window. Then I'm followed by someone in a black sedan and he grazes my bumper and doesn't stop. Then someone dumps a dead cat on my doorstep." I sucked in a deep breath and stared her in the eye. "And then there's you."

"Listen, JoLynne," Mandy said, patting my arm. "I know the timing is weird, but trust me, I'm not responsible for this."

I stared up at her. "Then who?"

Mandy said nothing.

I let out a ragged laugh. "I could use that wine now."

"Wine glasses in the kitchen?"

"Above the sink."

I watched her disappear into the kitchen and debated on whether I should call the police or not. Someone was messing with my head.

When Mandy emerged from the kitchen, she had a wine glass in one hand and a garbage bag in the other.

"What's the bag for?"

"I'm going to clean up the cat for you."

"You really don't have to do that."

"I know." Mandy paused near the front door. "Is there a Dumpster nearby? I don't want to throw it in your garbage can. Other animals will get in."

"There's one at the end of the back alley, about a half block away."

"Good. While I'm doing that, you need to check all your doors and windows, make sure they're locked." She gave me a smile. "Then sit back and enjoy your wine."

My eyes locked on the nearest window. "You don't think he'll try to break in, do you?"

"I honestly don't know." She opened the door. "I'll be back in five minutes. Lock the door behind me."

I did exactly that.

Sipping my wine, I headed upstairs and tried not to think about the dead cat. Mandy seemed awfully calm about it. Maybe too calm. She'd made no attempt to convince me to call the police.

My original doubts came flooding back.

Just who was Amanda Williams?

I was about to open my laptop and Google her name when I heard the sound of glass breaking. A silent alarm went off in my brain. I was supposed to check all the locks.

Idiot!

My rational side assured me I was imagining things. It had been a weird day after all. But the irrational side was set on high alert.

Then I heard footsteps.

Someone was in my house.

Downstairs, frenzied chaos erupted. Something crashed. More broken glass. Whoever was down there was trashing the place, and it was only a matter of time before they came upstairs.

Whipping around, I searched desperately for a place to hide. The bathroom was too small and the only place in my bedroom was the closet. It would be the first place the intruder looked.

Something creaked. I knew that sound. It was the loose step, the fifth one from the top. The intruder was heading upstairs.

I was trapped.

I yanked open my window, thinking I'd scream and alert my neighbors. When I noticed the roof a few feet below, I realized I could climb out the window and as long as I was careful, drop the ten or so feet to the ground.

I grabbed a pair of scissors and sliced open the screen. Pulling it aside, I threw one leg up and over. I eased myself onto the rain soaked shingles. Make no mistake, I was scared shitless. Acrobatics were never my forte. I could barely walk on a treadmill without falling off.

Behind me, I heard someone approaching my bedroom door. I knew that as soon as they found it locked, they'd know I was well aware of their intrusion.

And they were. Angry pounding slammed the door.

Taking a deep breath I crouched along the roofline and made my way to the edge, trying not to think of how high I was. My foot slipped and I let out a yelp. I slid about two feet before throwing myself against the shingles. One foot slid over the eaves trough. Panting, I stared at my scraped hands. They burned as if someone had poured iodine on open wounds.

Something crashed above me, probably my door.

I glanced up and saw the curtain fluttering half out the window. Nothing like leaving a neon sign to point the way. Whoever was in my room would know exactly where I was hiding. I had no choice. I inched my body over the eaves, dangled for a second, closed my eyes and let go.

When I hit the cold, sodden ground, air whooshed from my lungs and my right ankle twisted beneath me. I cried out in agony, rolled to my back and stared up at the roof. The angle made it impossible to see my bedroom window, but I imagined a gruesome masked face staring down at me with kind of a "heeere's Johnny" demented look, and a bloody axe in one hand.

I had to get up.

I struggled to my feet. The pain was excruciating and hot tears welled in my eyes. But I was alive.

I hobbled over to the fence and used it for support as I limped around the side of the house. I could barely breathe for fear that the intruder would come walking through the gate.

My mind flipped rapidly through the events of the past couple of days. The threatening emails. The face against the window. The sedan following me. The dead cat on my porch. Only one person in my life would have any reason to hold a grudge. Only one person had ever threatened me.

Mandy Williams.

She'd shown up so unexpectedly. She was staying in a hotel so close to my house, seemingly by coincidence. But I didn't believe in coincidences.

I paused at the gate, fumbling to find the latch.

Then I heard it. Rustling. Very close behind me.

Before I could turn around, a plastic bag swooped down over my head. I screamed. I kicked and lashed out. Gasping for air, I dug my fingers into the thick plastic, frantic to create a hole. The hands that tightened the bag around my neck were strong. Gloved. I could feel smooth leather and tried to sink my nails into them anyway.

I whipped around, but whoever had me in their grip moved with me. My arms flailed and I kicked. I tried to scream, but I couldn't get air.

My head pounded. So did my heart.

My vision blurred.

I needed air.

Everything spun and my legs gave out. My attacker stood behind me, keeping me up on my knees by fisting the bag around my neck. The heat from my breath clouded the plastic.

Everything grew hazy.

A drip of moisture beaded on the inside of the bag, clearing a path.

That's when I saw her.

She stood before me, a gun in her hand. It was pointed at me and I recalled the last words she'd said to me four years ago.

"I said you're a dead girl."

My attacker had a partner. Mandy.

Oh God. This was it. I was going to die.

I took one last short breath.

The sharp crack of Mandy's gun rang out

Then I died.

* * *

I can tell you from experience that dying is easy. You just close your eyes and give in. Give up. It's everything that comes right before dying that's hard. The pain, regret, grief. I'd barely begun to live and now it was over.

Then I woke up in the hospital. Alive. Breathing.

"What happened?" I asked the doctor.

"Someone tried to kill you," a voice said from the doorway. Mandy.

My heart fluttered and the monitor raced with it. "She shot me!"

"No," the doctor said. "Someone tried to strangle you."

It all came flooding back. The bag over my head. Mandy. The gun. "But she had a partner who—"

"Don't talk, JoLynne, just listen. I can explain everything." Mandy tugged a chair close to the bed and sat down. "Remember when we were kids, when I caught you and Jackson beneath the bleachers?"

"Yeah, you were jealous."

Mandy nodded. "I was stupid back then. And very emotional." She took a deep breath. "I was also very psychic."

I snorted. "So psychic that you couldn't tell Jackson was a sleaze?"

"I had to work with what I saw. And that day under the bleachers I saw you dying. Exactly like what happened tonight." She massaged her head. "Problem was I didn't know where, when or who would try to kill you. As I got older, the visions grew rarer."

I swallowed hard. "I saw you with a gun. Aimed at me."

Mandy reached into her jacket pocket. "I'm licensed to carry." She held up a badge.

"You're a cop?"

"I figured I should put my visions and instincts to good use."

"Why didn't you tell me? Why all the lies?"

"I knew someone would attack you, JoLynne. I knew I'd meet you before that happened. That's what I saw in my vision." She sighed. "But I wasn't completely sure who would come after you. I never saw a face in my vision."

A face.

Suddenly, I recalled the moments before I heard the gunshot. My attacker was behind me and there was an instant, a flash, when I saw his face. Dark, moustache, goatee…

"Julie Bell's boyfriend?" I said, uncomprehending. "Why would he want me dead?"

Mandy nodded. "Yes, he was her boyfriend."

"Was?"

"He's dead. I shot *him*."

I closed my eyes, struggling to make sense of everything. "But I never even met the guy. What would he have against me?"

"You caused him his career, JoLynne."

I gaped at her. "What are you talking about?"

"He had his sights set on a college football scholarship, but he lost the last school game."

"Jackson?"

"Jackson."

I thought of the boy who'd tried to grab a feel. I felt nothing for him except pity. Instead of moving on with his life, he'd let one moment fester in his mind until all he wanted was revenge.

"How did you know it would happen tonight?" I asked her.

"Your address is 5146."

"So?"

"When I drove by, I saw the five was missing."

"It blew off in last night's storm," I said, confused. "What's that got to do with it?"

"Your house number now reads 146." Mandy smiled faintly. "That's the number I kept seeing so many years ago when I saw your death."

"So when you saw my house number missing the five..."

"I knew it would happen tonight. I also figured out who would try to kill you."

"How did you know it was Jackson?"

"From the number."

When I gave her a blank look, she said, "146. One minute, forty-six seconds. That's how much time was left in Jackson's last high school game. The other team scored the final touchdown with one minute and forty-six seconds to spare."

I shuddered. "The paramedic said I was dead for one minute and forty-six seconds."

But I was the lucky one. Jackson hadn't survived.

I thought of how every choice we make, even ones from years ago, can affect our lives. If I'd made a different choice, maybe Jackson would still be alive. Maybe he wouldn't have turned out to be the psychotic stalker who'd nearly killed me. Or would he have just found someone else to blame?

Beware the past. Sometimes it can come back to haunt you.

Remote Control

(Finalist in 2008 Textnovel Contest)

The following novelette first appeared on Textnovel.com in late 2008. It was serialized, one chapter per day until finished. Remote Control is based on a short story of the same title that I wrote back in 1987, back when I wished to become a published author. Be careful what you wish for…

* * *

"Be careful what you wish for," they say, but for forty-four-year-old Harold Fielding, who unfortunately isn't one to listen to such good advice, those words will come back to haunt him.

Harold—*Harry*—always rebels against the norm. In fact, he says, "Wishes are like saying grace—something to be said before every meal." So he wishes at least five times a day, while growing exceedingly fat.

However, good ole Harry has an excuse.

"If I wish hard enough," he tells his wife Beatrice, "my wishes will eventually come true."

Harry's a TV fanatic and, surprisingly, fairly intelligent. He spends about ten hours a day parked in front of his ten-year-old Sanyo television with the remote control in hand, while watching shows on just about everything. The next day, he can tell you all about it; his recall is nearly perfect.

He never once contemplates actually working a forty-hour week and *earning* money. He's already maxed out the VISA and MasterCard, plus a small bank loan that Beatrice knows nothing about. And now he's waiting for his fortune to fall in his lap. Sadly, there's no room there, so whatever good luck finds him usually ends up in a puddle on the floor.

Harry's good with puddles. He's a plumber by trade, when he bothers to do a job. The truth is, he's been having trouble maneuvering under kitchen sinks; his stomach keeps getting in the way. Six months ago, he was depressed, which made him eat more. He'd almost lost faith that there is something better for him…somewhere…out there, and then fate stepped in.

After a chance run-in with an old classmate (Harry nearly knocked him down a flight of stairs when they passed on a landing), who happens to be very wealthy and who recommends one book, Harry's life changes forever.

The Secret sits on the shelf behind the toilet. Harry reads it while relieving himself of the pounds of food he's eaten each day. Since he's always there a while, he can usually get through five or six pages a visit.

"I've read it now from beginning to end at least five times," he boasts to his friends.

Of course, he hasn't quite figured out that one must work towards receiving the good things in life, whether by deed or thought. He just figures that if he wishes for something, he'll attract it. Eventually.

Be careful what you wish for, Harry.

* * *

On this fateful Friday night, Harry is sitting in his favorite recliner, the one with the sagging springs and torn leather footrest. He scowls at the television and balances a bowl of popcorn on his gargantuan stomach. Not an easy task.

"I wish to be rich and famous," he says, just as he does at least twice a day. A handful of greasy popcorn follows and his stomach rumbles in rebellion.

Harry wants everything out of life—recognition, an inexhaustible supply of money and the perfect family to share it with.

He glances over his shoulder at his wife. Beatrice is ironing his work shirt for tomorrow, a pinched expression on her face. He studies her for a moment. She's wearing her regular work outfit—a skirt and jacket in dove gray. *It would look great,* he thinks, *if she was twenty years younger.* Beatrice is thirty-nine. *And why won't that woman do something with her hair?* Beatrice has grown out all the blond hair color he likes. It's now a rusty gray, which she twists into a lump at the back of her head and fastens with one of those clamp thingies.

"You finished work early," she says without looking at him.

"It was an easy job."

Harry lets out a resounding belch in *b-minor*. The ominous sound is followed by a crescendo of sour pepperoni breath. It reminds him that there's still a half bag of mini pepperoni in the fridge.

Beatrice looks up. "Why not take on a few jobs a week, Harry? We could use the money."

She's holding her breath. He knows this because when she says *money*, it sounds like *buddy*.

"You're making enough for us to get by on, Bea," he says. "'Sides, I'm waiting for my lucky streak to kick in." He doesn't want her to ask why he's been taking a hundred dollars out every week. "You have faith in me, dontcha?"

Beatrice returns to her ironing with a loud sniff. She's annoyed. He can tell.

"It's gonna happen soon," he says, more to himself. "I can feel it. My luck's gonna change, and when it does, you'll be sorry for doubting me." He laughs. "And I'll say, 'I told you so.'"

He pushes the nearly empty popcorn bowl onto the end table beside his recliner and leans forward, grunting and shifting, trying to right the recliner. Finally, the footrest kicks into place. Then, with a deep breath, he grasps the arms of the recliner and throws his body forward and upward, and—*ta-da!*—we have lift off. Harold Fielding is standing.

With huffing breaths, he lumbers toward Beatrice.

* * *

"He's one step from the grave," her mother had told her just last week. And Beatrice has to agree.

She hears his heavy breathing moving closer but doesn't want to look at him. She doesn't want to see her reflection in his eyes, to know that her dull brown eyes rested in emaciated pits of shadowed skin, caverns that bespoke of countless sleepless nights.

It's Harry's fault. He snores loud enough to wake the dead. Sometimes he stops breathing for so long that she holds her own breath so she can listen. *Is he dead?* And every time, she jerks when a gasping, strangled choke rises from the depths of Harry.

She lifts her chin and finally looks at him. Her husband. The man she married over twenty years ago. *'Til death do us part.'* She scowls. *Well, how long is that going to take?* And as quickly, she takes it back.

Harry wasn't always like this. When she had married him, he had a bright future ahead of him and plenty of plans. They were going to build their own home, have three children and live in style. None of these dreams have come to fruition. The house they started building collapsed into a sinkhole when it was nearly completed. They had one daughter who moved out the day she turned eighteen and is now backpacking across Europe with a known drug dealer named Felipe. And as for living in style…?

She glances around the sad looking room. The sunflower wallpaper—circa 1970s—is peeling in long banana peel strips from the walls in the kitchen area. The dinette set is something they found on

71

Kajiji.com, purchased from a couple who were moving to Toronto. Harry has already broken two of the four chairs.

In the living room, the matching couch and armchair in pastel periwinkle sink so low to the ground that it looks as if they will get sucked into the floor and earth below. Another sinkhole perhaps? A wayward spring sometimes jabs Beatrice in the thigh when she sits in the armchair, and the cushion is as flat as a pancake. Harry's girth has taken care of that.

As her husband approaches, his massive belly flops over his pants and appears below the hem of his t-shirt. The waistband of his dirty track pants disappears beneath the drooping mass of dough-like flesh that hangs below his crotch. Oh, and there's his bellybutton. You could hide a bar of soap in *that*.

Harry's limbs are short and thick, tapering at the wrists and ankles, then flaring out into misshapen hands and feet that are always swollen and red. He scuffles and shuffles rather than walks, stopping to catch his breath every so often. Think of a gigantic Galapagos tortoise moving across the sand and you'll get the picture.

"Our savings is nearly gone," she says softly.

* * *

The only sound in the room is a ripping fart that Harry forces out as he passes her. He's been into the mini pepperoni sticks again, with a platter of eggs, it seems—by the noxious potpourri that simmers in the air.

"Maybe you can teach some extra classes at the college," he replies.

Beatrice bites her tongue. She already works full time teaching at an elementary school, plus she teaches the occasional adult class at Grant MacEwan. The college is already booked for courses for the next six months.

"I really think it's time you find more work," she persists.

"I wish you'd stop saying that."

He moves to the fridge, grabs another beer and waddles back to his recliner. He wipes his perspiring brow with the back of a chubby hand. His fingers look like sausages ready to explode from their casings. Then he reaches into the bowl of popcorn, flops back into his chair and picks up the remote control, thereby completing his exercise regime.

Beatrice clamps her mouth shut.

When is the last time I saw him without that godforsaken remote control in hand?

She remembers. Last spring, they'd taken a plane trip to New Brunswick to visit Harry's ailing mother. It wasn't a cheap trip either; they had to pay for three seats—two for Harry.

72

And how long has it been since we've gone to a movie?

The last time, poor Harry wedged himself into the theatre chair so tightly that it took Beatrice, three attendants and some of that fake butter topping to dislodge him. On the drive home, she saw him wipe his fingers over his greasy jeans and lick each plump digit. It was obscene.

She misses the old Harry. The slimmer one.

When's the last time he kissed me or told me he loves me? How long's it been since we made love?

She shakes her head. Sex is completely out of the question. The last time they tried, she ended up with a dislocated hip and two fractured ribs, not to mention acid reflux symptoms that lingered for days afterward. They even tried to be adventurous, with her on top, but that only made things difficult to locate, and the last thing Beatrice wanted to do was go digging around under the sweaty layers of stomach and between Harry's cellulite-dimpled, thunderous thighs. Plus Harry can't lie on his back for long anyway. He might pass out.

So why does she stay with him? After all, their daughter is grown and has flown the coop, leaving behind a tired old hen and an obese rooster who has no more "cock-a" in his "doodle-do".

She watches him now, a longing in her heart, wishing so desperately that he would return to the Harry she once admired and loved. Can it be that *that* man is gone permanently?

* * *

Beatrice recalls the day they were married.

The wedding was simple and sweet, and it took place a few months after college. Harry, decked out in a three-piece Armani suit that he'd borrowed from his brother, looked like the popular football jock that he was; Beatrice, wearing an elegant white dress cut low in the back, was the class valedictorian. She'd been so happy back then…and so in love. And Harry? Why, he'd literally swept her off her feet in a short five months.

Now he can barely lift his own feet.

They'd had such innocent dreams for their future together. She was going to teach wonderful, sweet children to read and write, maybe even homeschool their three equally wonderful and sweet offspring. Harry would own a plumbing company, hiring at least ten contractors, and they'd specialize in new homes. They'd target all the local builders and coax them with special deals. They'd all make a fortune.

But instead, reality had given her a classroom of unruly, spoiled children, a hectic schedule and one child of her own whom she'd had no time to homeschool. Harry's company lost customers daily because of his poor work ethic and the three contractors he'd hired last fall had all quit. Better pay elsewhere, they'd all said.

Beatrice catches sight of her reflection in the mirror above the dinette table. *What happened to me?*

Her thin lips are pursed in discontent as she flicks a look over her shoulder and stares at the protuberance in the recliner. *Things have got to change around here,* she thinks.

She hangs Harry's shirt over a wooden chair. "Goodnight, Harry." She pauses in the doorway.

In answer, her husband of twenty years points the remote at the television and switches channels.

Beatrice can't take much more of this.

She turns away. I wish that things would change.

Be careful what you wish for, Beatrice.

* * *

On this night—the night that '*IT*' happens—the weather takes on the frightening quality of an orchestra gone awry. A merciless, miasmic symphony of heat and humidity is brewing, churning the heavens into a hazy, hellish hue of burnt amber. Bitter black clouds as dense as tar pits clash overhead. Hot rain is spat out, a trumpeting torrent that splatters and spreads into running rivers, flooding the grass and streets. Jagged lightning spears are thrown down to earth, landing with precision in a field of sleeping cattle, then on a power line, causing the lights in Harry's rented abode to flicker. Thunder booms through the tiny two-bedroom house and an enraged wind drums on the doors, windows and the stove vent.

A pile of long overdue bills that Beatrice has left on the coffee table flutters to the ground, caught in a fluted draft that seeps under the front door and across the living room, and Harry shivers. The electricity in the air makes the hairs on his arms stand at attention.

"Goddamn storm," he mutters.

He knows that Beatrice is probably tossing and turning in the bedroom down the hall, but he isn't finished keeping his ever-vigilant watch of the small screen before him. There's fifteen minutes left of the hockey game and he's got a vested interest in the score. He's wagered a thousand dollars he took in increments of one hundred from their savings. One thousand dollars for the home team to win.

And he has a feeling…

The doorbell rings. His pizza is here.

He pays the delivery guy, who yawns sleepily and hands him the two-for-one box.

"Keep the change," Harry says, handing the guy a twenty.

The man gives him a scowl. "Thanks, buddy. I may be able to pay for the gas with that…uh," he looks at the receipt, "forty-eight cents."

Harry closes the door and waddles back to his chair, clutching the pizza box like an excited child holding a Christmas present. He opens the box, inhales about a thousand calories in one breath and downs a pizza in record time. He's starting on the second one when something crackles.

Harry jumps. "What the—?"

The lights wink again. Off, on.

"There'd better not be a power failure," he yells at the television.

The game is in the final minute.

"Come on! Get the goddamn puck, you assholes. Now, shoot it!"

He holds his breath, watching as the tiny puck on the screen glides across the ice toward the net.

Closer…closer…

* * *

Without warning, the TV goes fuzzy. Static hisses at him and Harry hisses back.

"Ssson-of-a-bitch!"

He changes channels with the remote, but every channel shows the same gray, stagnant static, so he clicks back to the game. Still nothing.

Harry heaves himself from the recliner, then pauses to catch his breath.

This is not the time for the stupid TV to act up.

Harry needs to know the score. He has to know if he's just made them ten thousand dollars richer, or if he'll have to find a way to cover his tracks—and hide the money loss.

"Aw, for crying out loud! I wish to God I knew the score."

With the remote control in one hand, he approaches the television with trepidation. He pushes the channel up button, and as his other hand—or fist, actually—makes contact with the box, he switches the channel back to the hockey game. Simultaneously and unbeknownst to Harry, a bolt of lightning sears the cable dish on his roof and a surge of electricity races down through the wiring and into his old television.

He feels a minor tingling sensation in his fingertips. Then a sharp jolt of pain courses up his arm.

"Beatrice!" he yells.

His voice sounds funny, as if he's in a deep cavern. His vision blurs and darkness wraps him in a cloak of oblivion. Sounds fade in and out, waves of voices on a restless sea.

The TV must be back on, his subconscious tells him.

He blinks. Then he gasps. *What was that?*

A face swims in front of him, too large for the television. A man's face. He has dark blue hair.

That's not right, he thinks.

He blinks again. And glimpses a crowd of people hovering over him.

Am I dead?

His vision clears and beyond the crowd, he sees hundreds—no, *thousands*—of screaming people.

"Where the hell am I?" he bellows.

But Harry knows exactly where he is.

* * *

He is standing now—after much assistance—and as he gazes across the stadium, his eyes rest on the hockey net at the other end of the ice rink. The home team is just setting up for a power play. The *same* scenario he's already witnessed at home, while sitting in his recliner with his popcorn and beer.

"Excuse me," a woman says beside him. "This is yours."

She presses a small black object into his hands. Harry's remote control.

He's stunned. And very confused. "But how did you...?"

"You dropped it when you fainted."

"I fainted?" He rubs his forehead, squinting as a sudden pain flashes through his temples.

Well, this is just wrong. I, Harold Abner Fielding, do not faint.

While he tries to make sense of it all, his hands habitually caress the remote control buttons. When he grazes the volume button, he applies more pressure than he initially intends. The result nearly makes him pee his pants. The volume in the arena increases.

"Must be a coincidence," he mumbles.

He pushes the volume decrease button and the surrounding sounds diminish to a bare whisper. Flabby fingers stroke his 'long lost lover', pressing the mute button. The arena is eerily silent, yet all around him, people go through the motions of screaming, jumping up from their chairs, stomping their feet and whistling at the dueling hockey teams. It reminds him of those old black and white silent pictures with the incomparable Charlie Chaplin.

He laughs, but no sound is emitted from his throat.

"You suck!" he silently yells at the guy beside him.

The guy gives him a nasty scowl.

Apparently, the remote only gives Harry the effects. Everyone else hears just fine.

Experimenting more, he presses the rewind button. It's a hysterically funny sight watching people move backwards, only slightly slower than normal. He glances at the woman behind him and immediately wishes he hadn't. She is regurgitating an all-beef hotdog smothered in mustard and onions.

His stomach heaves, so he turns around and resumes fiddling with the remote. Fast forward gives him the expected results. The channel buttons do nothing that he can see.

Distracted by this unexpected turn of events, he halfheartedly watches the final minutes of the game. As the puck makes its way across the center line, he catches sight of the "memory" button on the remote.

"Now what does a remote have to remember?"

He pushes it.

* * *

Zzzz-zap!

A blinding flash of light pierces his eyes and he clamps them shut. When he opens them, he finds that he is standing next to the television in his stuffy two-bedroom rental. The remote control is at his feet and a burnt plastic odor lingers in the air.

What the hell just happened here?

He shakes his head, trying to free the cobwebs of his mind. He obviously imagined everything.

Good God, Harry. You're losing it, buddy.

He laughs. It starts off as a self-deprecating chuckle, then bursts into a full blown Jell-O belly laugh. Above his own laughter, he hears a thunderous cheering. The hockey game is in the last three minutes and the crowd is screaming wildly.

The puck inches near the net, and Harry sees imaginary dollar signs. His bet is going to pay off.

"Shoot!" he screams, trying not to think of what just happened.

The puck hits the side of the goal net and ricochets between one player's feet, and the buzzer sounds. Game over. The home team has lost.

And so has Harry. He's just lost one thousand dollars.

He lets out a cry of frustration. "Goddamn losers!"

Leaning over—which in itself is a huge undertaking of clumsy choreography, a few squats and grunting wheezes—Harry finally retrieves the remote control from the floor. He places a hand on the top of the television, to steady himself as he rises and at the same time he changes channels with the remote.

In the barest blink he recognizes a documentary on the Arctic.

The next nanosecond, icy water engulfs him and his head dips beneath a watery grave. Pushing to the surface, he flounders and screams. "Help me!"

But there is no other sign of life, and his own is crawling out of him in an icy blue trail.

Jesus Christ, I'm drowning!

He almost opens his right hand. And then he remembers. *The remote.*

Teeth chattering, he prays harder than he's ever prayed. "Please let this work. Please!"

He can barely feel his death-tinged fingers, yet he manages to cradle the remote in one hand as he pokes at the memory button.

He's instantly transported back to the safety of his living room and the clock on the wall tells him that the game ended about ten minutes ago. He could have shrugged this off as another 'zoning out' period except for two things—he is ice cold and dripping wet. Arctic water pools around his feet, while his teeth continue clattering loud enough to wake the living dead.

Or Beatrice, at the very least.

She appears on cue in the doorway, her weary eyes blinking to adjust to the light, her arms folded across her tattered gray housecoat. It was blue when he'd bought it for her last Christmas.

He watches her, wondering how long it will take her to realize that all is not right.

"Harry?" Blink…yawn…gasp! "What in God's name is going on here?"

* * *

Beatrice searches the room for the source of the water. There's no leak in the ceiling and the kitchen sink isn't overflowing. *So where'd all that water come from?*

Her eyes narrow in suspicion as she steps closer to Harry. "Did you go outside?"

It's the only thing that makes any sense to her, yet the rain had stopped about half an hour ago.

Harry gives her his *'you're so dense'* glare, then releases an exasperated sigh. "Of course I didn't go outside."

"Then why are you standing in the living room soaking wet?"

Ignoring her, he pushes past and waddles toward the bathroom.

"Just like a man," she mutters. "Avoid the question and run away."

While he's gone, Beatrice cleans up the water on the hardwood floor. She searches for the remote control so she can turn off the TV, but it's nowhere to be found.

"Harry?" she calls out. "Where's the remote?"

He appears beside her, the remote firmly grasped in one hand.

She holds out her hand.

"I'm not done watching TV," he says.

"But it's almost eleven-thirty."

He looks at her, raises his eyebrows. "And your point is?"

"You always go to bed by eleven when you have a job in the morning."

"I know." He glances at the television. "But I have a plan that is sure to make us rich."

She rolls her eyes. Another one of Harry's 'plans'. Oh goodie.

"I have an idea," he continues, "that'll make you wish you'd never doubted me."

"What *I* wish," she snaps, "is that you'd stop all your wishing once and for all. *I* wish that you'd stop pressuring me to work more hours and figure out a way to fix this mess we're in. In fact, I wish that you'd just leave me alone!"

Beatrice turns on one heel, but his portentous words follow her.

"Be careful what you wish for, dear Bea."

* * *

Harry is desperately afraid. Afraid that he's imagined everything, that he's had a stroke or something and temporarily blacked out. Terrified in a way that makes his heart race with anticipation that maybe, just maybe, he hasn't dreamt it up after all.

There's only one way to find out.

It's now just past midnight and Harry has changed his clothes, toweled off his hair, and his skin has returned to its normal color of malnourishment. Leaning forward as far as his tire tube belly allows, he sits in his recliner and contemplates how he can use his new best friend to make all his wishes come true. His pudgy hands are glued to the remote, as if his life depends on its close proximity.

"Okay, RC," he says. "Let's see what you can really do."

Now don't forget how smart Harry is. He's already thought this through. If everything that happened was real, then he has somehow found a kind of portal. And portals can be very useful—if one can figure out how to use them.

"I was transported to the same hockey game I was watching on TV," he says. "I was actually there. Then I changed channels and went to the Arctic, just like the documentary." He shivers. "Bad move there."

Needing something safe to test his theory on, he channel surfs.

"There!"

The screen shows dozens of digital cameras, flat screen TVs and laptops. Tonight's news is featuring a piece on the grand opening of a Best Buy store in southeast Edmonton. According to the reporter, the grand opening sale is on '*NOW*'.

"Then *NOW* is the best time," he says with a wry grin.

He never stops to wonder what will happen if he selects a commercial that has been pre-recorded in a store that is now closed. But he does do two things. He wishes and waits.

Nothing happens.

"What the hell?"

He holds the remote out in front, points and changes channels quickly, from a beer commercial back to the Best Buy ad, wishing with all his might for fame and fortune.

Still nothing.

He turns the television off, then on, and tries again. Point...wish...click channel button.

Disappointed that he's still sitting in his chair, he says, "Why won't you work?"

Scowling, he scratches his chins and replays previous actions in his head, thinking of everything he could have possibly done.

Finally, he smiles. "Ah-ha! I touched the TV."

Thankful he hadn't reclined his chair, he begins to rock. One...two...three! Up he goes.

Weebles wobble, but they don't fall down.

As a last thought, he grabs a hooded jacket he'd flung over the couch earlier that day. He doesn't bother to zip it up—he couldn't have even if he wanted to. But he does pull the hood over his head and fastens the top snap under his chins.

He shuffles to the television and touches the faded black plastic. Making his wish, he switches back to the Best Buy commercial. In a single heartbeat, he sees his arm and hand disintegrate.

Then Harry vanishes completely.

* * *

He's staring into a pitch-black cave. It takes a few moments for his eyes to adjust, and when they do, he realizes that he's inside the Best Buy store—after closing. Not even a night janitor is around.

"It works!" He jerks as his voice echoes through the cavernous building with its high, open ceiling.

Harry is stunned. He's tempted to hit the memory button and return home to collect his thoughts. But then it hits him; he should be collecting something else. He's standing in a store filled with expensive electronic equipment. Stuff worth thousands of dollars. Per shelf. Stuff he could keep—or sell. And best of all, there's no sign of a break-in, and there'll be no evidence of his departure.

He glances up, sees a security camera sweeping the area and pulls the hood tighter. "Security!"

Chuckling at his brilliance, he stares at his good friend RC and strokes the small black box. "Can I take really something back with me?" He remembers something. "Well, I brought back some of the Arctic Ocean, didn't I?"

Makes sense to him that objects can be transported just as easily as water.

"This'll be a reconnaissance trip," he decides, thinking of the movie Ocean's Eleven with George Clooney and a host of other big name actors. "It'll be a dry run, and I'll be Clooney."

He waddles down one aisle, grabs a Canon camera and wraps the strap around his neck. Then he shoves four small digital cameras into his jacket pockets, two per side. He grins. With a skip and a bounce in his step—well, as much as his three hundred and sixty pound frame will allow—he lumbers into a second aisle and scoops a laptop up with one hand.

Then he sees it, the most wondrous thing in the store.

A forty-two inch Panasonic flat-screen TV.

Shuffling toward his treasure, he practically salivates at the sight, and he makes a decision that will make one of his routine wishes finally come true. He hugs the flat-screen, squeezes his eyes shut and says a quick prayer.

"There's no place like home," he says.

He tries to click his heels, but his marshmallow thighs won't let him.

So he presses the memory button on the remote instead.

* * *

Harry stands motionless in his living room. His pockets are stuffed with stolen loot and the flat-screen he's holding makes his arms ache. He rests his new treasure on the couch and groans at the physical exertion. He stares at it and his jaw drops. A drip of drool slides from the corner of his mouth, down his chin and disappears into the unshaven folds of his face.

Harry's eyes widen in comprehension. "I did it."

He realizes something and puffs up his already expansive girth. He's no longer just Harold Fielding, plumber extraordinaire. Now he's a thief, a criminal, a wanted man.

He grins and holds himself more erect. It feels good to be wanted, to be somebody special. A tingle of anticipation gives him a delicious shiver as he thinks of the police investigation that will follow. They'll wonder how someone got in and out without touching the doors or windows.

They'll think I'm amazing.

He empties his pockets. "And I am amazing."

He can't believe he made away with it all. And he didn't even set off the Best Buy's alarm.

Harry gasps. Maybe the press will give me a special nickname.

"Maybe they'll call me *The Disappearing TV Thief.*"

Laughter escapes from his mouth, his bulky belly doing 'the wave' as it ripples with each laugh.

He covers his mouth with fat fingers.

What to do now…

He must have an excuse for having all this state-of-the-art equipment. Now what can he tell Beatrice? Maybe an uncle passed away and left him—no, that wouldn't do. Beatrice knows he doesn't have an uncle.

He snaps his fingers as an idea hits him.

Harry grins. "I'll tell her I won everything. In a lottery."

She'll never know the truth. She'd never approve of it.

Suddenly, Harry hears a sound that makes his heart stop.

Footsteps.

Good God, Beatrice is awake!

* * *

Beatrice peeks around the corner and sees Harry sitting in his recliner, his eyes wild looking and his face flushed. He's wearing a jacket, which is odd since it's the middle of the night and the house is toasty.

"Harry, what's wrong? Are you ill?"

"No."

She notices that he's covered in an oily sheen of perspiration. "Should I call 911?"

He shakes his head, his breath coming in quick pants. "Bad dream."

Beatrice looks at him for a long moment. "Come to bed, Harry. You're going to be too tired to work tomorrow." She glances at the clock on the wall. "Or should I say, today. It's almost two."

"I'll be up in a minute." He gives her an innocent looking smile and a sweat bead rolls down the side of his face, cascades down his three chins and drops on his shirt.

Her eyes narrow. What's he up to?

She follows his gaze to the closet. "What's in there, Harry?"

"Where? What are you talking about?"

"What are you hiding in the closet?" she demands.

He shoves himself from the chair, wobbles, and says, "I'm not hiding a thing."

She doesn't believe him. He's too interested in that darned closet. Can't keep his eyes off it.

She walks toward the closet door with the intention of exposing Harry's secret. Probably half a dozen assorted flavors of potato chips and a bulk package of chocolate bars.

She scowls. Or more dirty magazines.

She'd already found his stash in the garage and made him burn them outside in the fire pit.

Men!

"Really, Bea," he insists, "it's nothing. I can't help where I was looking."

She hesitates in front of the closet door.

"Why don't we go upstairs," Harry says. "We can have some fun."

He raises and lowers his brows in an attempt to be suggestive, but Bea isn't interested in his idea of fun, the kind that always leaves her unfulfilled, with cracked ribs.

"No, Harry. I'm more interested in what's in here."

She reaches out a hand, touches the doorknob and turns it.

* * *

The closet holds all that once was, or once could have been. When she opens the door, two tennis balls—still bright yellow—roll between her feet. The rackets hang on the inside of the door, never used. Inside and to the left is Harry's barely used golf bag. Beside it are three burgundy suitcases for the many fabulous vacations that never happened. Cardboard boxes filled with Harry's extra plumbing gear are stacked to just under the clothing bar on the right side. Behind all this are more boxes and a pile of wool blankets and beach towels—for the picnics they never went on anymore.

Her fingers trail across the suitcases. She wonders if she'll ever use them again.

"So what didn't you want me to see in here, Harry?"

"Nothing, dear. Really." Harry's voice is thin, nervous.

She glances over her shoulder at him. "Then why are you so nervous, *dear*?"

Harry releases a long sigh. "I-I just realized how messy it was in there. You asked me to clean it up on my day off. I forgot to do it. Don't be upset with me, Bea. I'll do it right after work tomorrow. I promise."

She cocks her head. Maybe she's been too hard on him. Maybe he can't help that work's been slow.

"Maybe I can do it—"

"No!" Harry moves to her side and firmly closes the closet door. "*I'll* do it. I made a promise to you. I don't want you lifting a finger. The stuff in there is heavy, and most of it'll be going to the junkyard. The rest I'll store in the basement, or at least make a bit neater in the closet. Let me do that for you." He gives her a pleading look.

Well, I can't hurt his feelings by telling him no, now can I?

"Fine. You take care of it. I have enough to clean anyway." She gives him a tired look. "I sure wish we could hire someone to clean the house once a month. My joints are aching all the time and I can't wash the floors like I used to." Her voice fades with yearning. "I wish you were making more money."

Will he get the hint?

Harry's eyes have a strange glimmer in them. "I'm working on it, Bea. Believe me."

She almost does. Almost.

"I'll believe it when I see it," she says sadly.

* * *

Harry tiptoes into the living room the following morning and heads for the closet, hoping and praying that he hasn't dreamt it all, that there really are cameras and a flat-screen TV stashed behind the boxes. He flicks a look over his shoulder. Beatrice is in the shower, but he can't be too careful.

He opens the door and grunts as he shifts the top three boxes.

There! Right behind them is the top of the flat-screen.

He lets out a whoop. "Ho-ly shee-it." He covers his mouth, but not before a giggle escapes.

Returning the boxes to their original positions, he quickly shuts the door. As soon as Beatrice leaves for work, he'll move them to the basement.

Harry checks his clipboard to see what appointments he has booked. He's too keyed up to even think of going to work. Last thing he wants to do is wedge himself under some old lady's sink and unclog a drainpipe that she's clogged up by washing her rapidly thinning hair and her five dogs and six cats. Not to mention, she's probably hawked in it every morning to clear up a phlegmy throat.

What he really wants to do is check to see what's on TV.

"Let's see what's on the tube," he says, settling in his chair.

He picks up the remote and turns on the television, wishing it was the brand new one sitting in the back of the closet. He scrolls through the channels until he comes to the guide. There's a game show on in a few hours.

"That won't do," he realizes. "I'd just show up. They wouldn't just let me play."

The cursor hovers over Channel 78. Oprah will be on later in the day.

Harry chuckles. "Like to see Oprah's face if I just popped up on that couch beside her."

No, the queen of daytime TV will have to wait. Maybe once he's rich and famous she'll invite him to be a guest on her show. Bea too. That would sure score brownie points with her.

He starts channel surfing. Maybe something exciting will catch his eye.

And something does.

* * *

Global TV flashes a *"BREAKING NEWS"* banner.

"Sometime early this morning," news anchor Bill Humphrey says, "the new Best Buy store located in southeast Edmonton was broken into and robbed. We have Desiree Montgomery standing by."

The camera cuts to an attractive young woman with sleek blond hair. She's standing inside the store, right about the place where Harry had 'landed'.

"What can you tell us, Desiree?" Bill asks.

"Well, police don't have much to go on at this time, Bill. As you can see behind me, officers are still dusting for fingerprints. However, they don't think they'll find anything they can distinguish from the thousands of people who have walked through these doors since the store opened three days ago."

"Do they know how the thief broke in?"

"That's the strange thing. Police have ruled out entry by either the front or back door. Outdoor security cameras show no movement in front of either. Right now they're looking into the possibility that the thief waited inside the store until it closed, then somehow made it past security with the goods in hand when the store opened."

"I understand an interior security camera caught the man on tape," Bill says.

The screen splits, showing Desiree on one side and a black and white video on the other.

Desiree smiles but her tone is serious. "There is some static just before we see the man. And just before he disappears. Because he wore a hood, the store's security camera was unable to fully capture his face, but authorities tell me they're analyzing the tape as we speak. For now, the identity of the Best Buy Bandit remains unknown."

And there it is—Harry's new superhero name.

85

The Best Buy Bandit.

Harry likes it. He can just picture future headlines: *Best Buy Bandit Strikes Again!*

"It's definitely a mysterious case," Bill says, the camera focusing in on his perfect smile. "Thank you, Desiree. The Best Buy Bandit is described as a heavyset male, approximately four hundred pounds."

Harry is pissed. The camera has added a hefty forty pounds, instead of the ten everyone talks about.

"No one knows how he broke in," Bill continues. "Or how he got out."

But Harry knows. And he isn't telling a soul.

* * *

Harry runs into a roadblock. Figuratively, that is.

He has a basement full of stolen loot, but no pawn shop will touch it. He hadn't though of that. With the fame of the Best Buy Bandit creating a wave of excitement across Edmonton, all pawn shops are on high alert, and Harry can't risk getting caught.

"Crap!" he mutters the following afternoon as he stares at the flat-screen TV.

Then he has an idea.

He brings the flat-screen TV upstairs, hooks it up and places the old TV on the passenger seat of his van. He'll take whatever he can get for that one. When Beatrice comes home after work, he has a lie all ready and waiting. He'll tell her he got an advance for a major contract today, and as a treat, he bought them a new TV.

"It'll be far more believable than winning a lottery," he says to his reflection in the flat-screen. "Bea will be so proud."

He grabs the shiny new remote control and is just settling into his recliner when it hits him. He can't get rid of the old TV. It's his money-making lifeline. His 'golden goose'.

"What the hell was I thinking?"

He gives the flat-screen a look filled with regret and yearning.

Twenty minutes later, the TVs are switched again, and all looks as it had.

"Maybe I can sell the flat-screen on Kijiji," he mutters.

But Harry's not stupid. The police will be monitoring Kijiji and the Bargain Finder.

He thinks of all the stolen stash hidden in his basement.

Useless. It's all useless.

The only thing he can do is wait until he takes a trip out of town.

So much for feeling lucky. Now Harry feels like he was duped.

"There's got to be a better way to do this. What I need is cold, hard cash. And lots of it."

But where does one find that on TV?

He flips open the TV guide and scours the listings.

"Money, money, money, I got love in my tummy," he sings.

Harry's forgotten the Sunday School lesson his mother had drilled into him when he was seven.

The love of money is the root of all evil.

All evil aside, Harry's mouth stretches into a slow smile when he reads tomorrow's schedule.

"Yee-ha," he says. "Thank God for repeats. I've struck gold."

* * *

Bea wakes up to a strange sound. It's morning and something is whistling.

Did Harry forget to unplug the kettle?

She clambers out of bed, throws a housecoat over her cotton nightgown and wanders into the bathroom. Harry is in the shower—whistling a merry tune.

"Harry?"

"I'll be out in a minute, Bea."

She studies him through the glass doors. The frosted glass distorts his body and for a moment, she thinks he's grown two heads. But no, he's brought a mirror into the shower.

"Are you shaving?" she asks in complete disbelief.

Harry rarely shaves. Heck, he is rarely up this early in the morning.

"Yes, I have a busy day ahead of me," he says. Then he goes back to his whistling.

Now Bea is ticked off. She has forty minutes to get ready for work.

"I need the shower, Harry."

"I'm almost done."

As she's brushing her teeth, Harry finishes up. He looks extremely happy as he steps out of the shower.

"What's going on?" she asks.

"I have a new work project today. One that should pay pretty good."

Bea turns away and rolls her eyes. "Really."

Harry tries to secure a towel around his waist but even the huge bath sheets she bought are too small. "You have your scrapbook class tonight, don't you?"

She studies him. "Why?"

Harry shrugs. "Just wondering. I'll be working late tonight."

Bea almost laughs. "Work? You? I'll believe it when I see it."

"Don't you need to have a shower?" Harry snaps before heading into the bedroom.

As she stands motionless in the bathroom, Bea's suspicion grows. Something isn't right with Harry. She knows it. All her years working with conniving students taught her one thing—how to spot a liar.

"Just what are you up to, Harold Fielding?"

* * *

"Fifteen minutes until I'm rich," Harry murmurs.

He's had a busy day unclogging Mr. McKinley's bathtub drain for the fifth time in the last month, then cleaning the drains over at the old folk's home, and finally fixing a broken water pipe in a new customer's basement.

Now he's home, grinning and pacing like a child eager for his first visit to the zoo.

He can't wait to wipe that irritating smirk off Bea's face. In fact, maybe he'll do more than that. Maybe he'll get rid of her once and for all. He could poison her. Or drown her in the bathtub.

"A rich man like I'll be deserves a better wife." He thinks of Donald Trump. "I'll get me a younger wife, one that doesn't nag me to death...one that looks like a model. Then I'll live in the lap of luxury."

Oh, yes, Harry can see it now. A new home—a mansion! A yacht or two. Trips to Paris, Greece, France...wherever he wants to go.

"And all the money I can hope for."

The clock ticks and he watches the minute hand. "Five more minutes."

"Harry?"

His body jerks toward the front door. "I thought you'd left, Bea."

"I had to put a load of laundry on," she said, shifting a flowered handbag to her shoulder. "Clothes don't wash themselves, you know."

He ignores the not-so-subtle dig. "I'm heading out in a few minutes."

From a window, he watches Bea walk down the sidewalk. He feels no sense of remorse that only minutes ago he was plotting her untimely demise. He loved Bea. Once. But things change. He's changed.

He puffs out his chest. "You'll be sorry you didn't have more faith in me."

The clock ticks to the final minute.

Harry smiles. Then he wobbles across the room, picks up the remote control and turns on the TV.

"It's time."

He checks the TV guide and switches to Channel 20. There's a commercial for Canadian Idol on, but he knows that won't make him rich. So he waits, his eyes lighting up at the thought of what he was about to do.

Finally, the hour-long show begins, a documentary that was filmed last year.

The host of the show comes onto the screen. He's a well-dressed man in his forties. He touches the security bars that separate him from a fortune, and turns a smile toward the viewing audience.

Harry gives him a nod. "Show me the money!"

"Welcome," the host says, "to Fort Knox, home of the United States Bullion Depository."

* * *

"The US stores a large amount of gold reserves here," the host says. "Currently there is close to 150 million ounces in this fortified vault. And today you are going to take a virtual trip inside."

Harry stands still, transfixed by the realization that within minutes, he'd become the richest man alive. If he were a cartoon figure, we'd see dollar signs rolling up into his eyes. *Ca-ching!*

"This vault is constructed of granite, steel and concrete," the host continues. "The blast-proof door alone weighs more than 20 tons. The high tech security system that is in place makes it impossible for anyone to get inside the vault."

At that, Harry laughs. "We'll see about that, now won't we?"

While the host launches into a boring history of Fort Knox, Harry rushes into the kitchen.

"This oughta do it," he says, grabbing two garbage bags.

He scurries back to the living room as fast as his rotund body allows. Wheezing, he gets there just in time to watch the vault door open, exposing thousands of gold mint bars stacked from floor to ceiling.

"Oh...my...God."

Nearly passing out, Harry grabs the back of the armchair for support.

"Only some of the gold is visible," the host says. "One must go through separate cells to view the full amount of gold stored here."

"I think what I see right now will do just fine." Harry reaches for the remote control.

Commercial break.

"Damn it!"

He stands in front of the TV, two garbage bags in one hand and the remote in the other. Waiting.

Another ad.

This time for feminine products—just what Harry needs.

"Oh, goody. A commercial for Always with wings." His eyes narrow. "Maybe Bea will buy some and fly away."

The host finally returns. He flashes his too-perfect smile at the camera, making Harry cringe. He's seen enough episodes of Extreme Make-Over to know veneers when he sees them.

"Now let's go see some gold," the man says.

Harry nods. "Yes, let's."

He knows that if he tries now, he'll be stuck outside a locked vault door. He needs a shot of the inside of the vault. That's when he'll make his move.

The host steps into the vault and the camera crew follow him inside.

Harry wastes no time. He switches channels, touches the TV, makes his wish, then switches back.

Poof! Harry vanishes, leaving behind an empty house.

Only it's not as empty as he thinks.

* * *

"Where'd you go, Harry?" Bea whispers from her hiding place.

She rubs her eyes and stares in shock at the place where her husband had been standing mere seconds earlier. Harry had vanished before her eyes.

"I must be dreaming," she says, stunned.

She pinches herself. It hurts.

This is no dream, Beatrice Fielding. Maybe you never should have come back.

But she has.

Sensing that something was going on with Harry, Bea had decided to forgo an evening of scrapbooking with her friends. She had crept into the house through the back door and stood around the corner near the front door, peeking out every now and then to watch Harry's every move.

But what I saw is impossible.

Nothing makes sense.

Why did you get up early, Harry? What on earth were you doing watching TV when you said you had a big project?

Bea frowns. "And how did you disappear like that?"

She is tempted to search the living room for clues, but something makes her stay where she is.

Fear.

Bea is terrified of what she's seen, what she doesn't understand.

"How can you do this…thing, disappear like that? It's not normal. You've changed, Harry."

Peering around the corner again, she studies the spot by the TV. She thinks about Harry's laziness, his lies and his insulting treatment of her. She'd married him, 'for better or worse'.

"This is definitely the 'worse' part."

She pictures him standing by the TV. She couldn't see exactly what he was doing, but one second he was there in his rolls of flesh, the next he was gone. All three hundred and sixty pounds of him.

Bea's hands are shaking, so she brings them to her chest and clasps them hard against her, all the while staring at her wedding ring. The simple gold band no longer represents the promise of love and happiness. It means entrapment, pure and simple. It's a noose tightening around her throat until she can no longer breathe.

Oh God! I wish I could escape this life. I'd do anything to be free. Anything!

By now, Bea should know to be more careful with her wishes.

* * *

Harry can't believe his good fortune. His luck has finally changed. He's standing in the main vault with enough gold around him to pave the city streets of Edmonton. And it's all his. At least, as much as he can carry.

He opens up one of the garbage bags. "I'll fill these, then be on my way."

The first gold bar he reaches for makes him pause. He strokes the cool, smooth surface with his fingertips, all the while imagining a suit made with gold threads. Grinning, he picks it up. It's a bit heavier than he expected, but he manages to get it into the bag. He reaches for another.

By the time he has seven bars in the bag, he realizes his mistake.

"I'll never be able to carry a full bag. Besides, it'll rip before I get it off the ground."

It seems that stealing gold from Fort Knox is going to be more difficult than he has anticipated.

He removes two bars from the bag. Then he checks his watch. "Bea won't be home for at least two hours. That'll give me plenty of time to make a few trips, a few gold bars at a time."

He tests the bag, lifting it a few inches off the ground. "Home, RC."

With a press of the memory button he finds himself back in his living room. "I did it!"

He tries to do a victory dance, but the heavy bag knocks him off balance and he stumbles into the coffee table and bangs his knee. Hobbling toward his recliner, he places the garbage bag with its golden treasure on the seat. "By the time I'm done, I'll have this room filled with gold."

He moves back to the TV and prepares for round two. As he switches channels, an angry voice behind him says, "What do you think you're doing?"

But Harry's already gone.

He's now standing in the centre of the main vault. It takes him a few minutes to calm his racing heart, and a bit longer before he realizes something is dreadfully wrong. Something more than having Bea walk in just as he vanishes into thin air.

Alarms are blaring.

"The alarm must be weight sensitive. I must have set it off when I took the gold."

But that's not his only problem. Harry is missing a very valuable object.

He stares at his empty hands.

"Oh shit, I dropped the remote."

* * *

Bea holds the precious remote control. At first, she doesn't comprehend its importance. All she knows is that Harry dropped it a split second before he disappeared again.

She steps away from the TV, but something makes her look back over her shoulder. "Harry?"

He has somehow been transported inside the television set. No! Not *in* it, but in the location where the current TV show was shot.

"What is that?" She leans closer. "Good God! He's surrounded by gold."

The words 'Fort Knox – United States Bullion Depository' scrolls across the screen.

"My God, Harry is trying to rob Fort Knox."

She begins to pace the room, struggling with thoughts of what she should do.

Should I call the police? Should I wait for him to return? What if he doesn't return?

The remote control draws her attention.

"This is some kind of teleportation device." She rubs her forehead, then pauses. "And I bet anything he needs it to come back."

She thinks of the words. *Remote…control.*

"Remote means separated or far removed in space, time or relation," she says. "Control means power or authority to guide someone or something."

She looks at the TV screen. She sees Harry turning around in slow circles, his hands over his ears to block the sound of the shrill alarm.

92

There is a terrified expression on his face, and he looks like he'll burst into tears at any second.

Bea crouches in front of the TV. Her husband peers up at her and she realizes that for a man with great memory recall, he's never once acknowledged how badly he's treated her.

"You've been controlling me for years, Harry. I think it's time for *you* to be...remote."

* * *

Harry is panting so rapidly he feels like he'll pass out. The alarm threatens to burst his ear drums.

"Think, Harry!"

His ticket home—his old pal RC—is on the living room floor in his house. In another country, for crying out loud. And he's sure he heard Bea say something just before he vanished.

Maybe she can see me, he thinks.

He has no idea how this part works.

Maybe I should've set up a video camera to tape the television.

"Maybe I never should've tried for the gold," he berates himself.

The alarm shuts off.

"Thank you, God."

He hears a dull thud. His heart begins to race as he realizes there's only one reason for the alarm to shut off. The police must have arrived, and any minute they're going to come swarming through the vault door to arrest him.

"They'll put me in jail," he cries. "I can't go to jail."

He realizes there's only one thing left to do. If in fact Bea can see him on the television, he must plead with her to push the memory button.

"Bea, if you can hear me, you've got to press the memory button on the remote control."

He hears more clanging on the other side of the vault door.

"Please, Bea. Push the memory button!"

Maybe she can't hear me.

The vault door lets out a hiss. It's about to open and when it does Harry's fate will be sealed.

"Bea! Press memory! We can go on holidays, buy a new house, anything you want."

Harry never even considers that his wife might have other plans—plans that don't include Harold Fielding and his gargantuan belly and his mean-spirited temper.

* * *

Bea watches her husband on the TV and carefully considers her options.

93

"Quick!" Harry cries out, quaking in fear. "You have to press the memory button!"

He looks pitiful on the screen. Small, weak, pathetic.

Bea's fearful expression begins to transform. Her lips curve upward into a slight smile and the twinkle returns to her eyes.

Behind Harry the vault door is opening.

"Bea!" he bellows. "Press the goddamn memory button!"

Her finger hesitates over the red button. One touch and Harry might come home.

"Hurry up, for God's sake!" Harry growls. "Why are you always so damned slow at everything? Move your fat ass!"

Even smart men can be stupid. And this time, Harry has pushed her too far.

Bea heaves a sigh. "So I have the fat ass, do I?"

Her finger moves to the top of the remote. The large button, upper right.

"Bea! Push the memory button or so help me I'll—"

She turns off the TV.

For ten minutes, Bea doesn't move. She just gazes into the blank screen of the old television, wondering about Harry's fate. She knows one thing for sure. Harry got his wish for fame and fortune. His infamy will send him to prison. His fingerprints all over the gold will keep him there for decades.

Let's hope Bea can live with what she's done.

The five gold bars she finds the next morning in the garbage bag on Harry's recliner might help.

As for Harry, he has finally learned the greatest lesson of all. All the wishing in the world can't bring you the kind of fame or fortune you desire. You've got to work hard for these.

What about you, dear reader? Are you wishing for something? For fame, fortune or freedom?

If so, just remember these words…

Be careful what you wish for. You just might get it.

94

Ouija

Last spring, while packing away my aunt's belongings at her lakeside cottage, I discovered this letter in a box of old party games…

* * *

February 13, 2004

To Whom It May Concern:

If you found this letter, it means I'm dead.

DEAD!

Plain and simple.

And if I'm dead it's not by natural causes, I can assure you. I'm writing in haste cause I know I don't got much time.

It's after me!

What, you're asking. Well, I'll tell you.

It all started with that gawdforbidden Ouija board. The board that my best friend and I found in her attic.

Liza and I had been friends and neighbors for more than 45 years. We even buried our husbands within 2 years of each other. And no, we didn't bury them in the backyard.

Let me make somethin clear, first off. I'm not crazy. I'm of sound mind. Maybe not sound body though. I'm not crazy and neither was Liza. I'm as sane as you, whoever is reading this, and what I'm about to tell you is true. TRUE! Not one word is a lie.

My phone rang a few nights ago.

"Liza," I said. "It's 3 o'clock in the gawddamn morning!"

"You gotta come over, Sharon. Quick!"

"Why do I have to come over now? Can't it wait until morning?"

There was silence.

I sat up in bed and turned on my lamp. "Liza, you there?"

"I hear voices," she whispered. "There's someone in my attic."

95

Liza sounded scared, more scared than I ever heard her before, and her voice gave me a chill up my spine.

"Maybe you should call the police," I said.

"No, it's not that kind of voice."

Aw crap! There was only one other kind of voice that Liza heard. Ghost voices.

"Be right over," I said.

Liza had been hearing ghost voices all her life. She heard when little Jimmy Barton called from Mr. Porter's well. The police found his body the next day. Jimmy had somehow fallen in and drowned…three days before. Liza also heard Mrs. Morgensteen calling to her one night to let her cats outside. When my friend got to the old lady's door, she could smell something rank and awful. The police found Mrs. Morgensteen dead on the floor. The newspapers said she had been dead almost a week.

Anyways, I have to tell you this so's you can see I'm telling the truth. So you'll believe me when I tell you what happened next.

After Liza called, I dressed quickly then stepped outside. There was a full moon and a fog had settled over our lane. I remember thinking how strange the weather was.

Ghost weather.

Crossing the street, I walked down the sidewalk to the corner. Liza lived less than a block from me. When I got to my friend's house, I saw her lights were out. Everything was black. The least she coulda done was put the porch light on for me. So in the glow of the moon I crept up toward her front door, not knowing if I should ring the bell or walk right in.

The door opened with a groaning creak and I jumped.

"Don't scare me like that!" I hissed, then stood with my mouth open.

Liza Plummer, from 1842 Walker Lane off Aurora Lake, looked like death warmed over. My friend's thin gray hair was a mess, her eyes were sunken in like she hadn't slept in a month and she was wearing her natty old housecoat, the one she refused to throw away.

Liza's a packrat. Can't let go of anything.

"Its coming from the attic," she whimpered.

We closed the front door and made our way upstairs. In the ceiling of the hallway there was a trap door. That's how you got to her attic. Using a broom, we hooked the rope handle and pulled it toward us. The trap door opened and—lo and behold—a set of steps appeared, ending almost two feet off the ground.

Now Liza and I, we aren't in the prime of life anymore. She's 58 and I'm 61. So getting up the first step took a bit of trying. Liza refused to go ahead of me so I put my foot in her hands and she boosted me to the first step. Then I leaned down and hauled her up behind me. A few minutes later, we were up and poking our heads into the pitch-black attic.

"Dontcha got a light in here?" I asked her.

She reached into her housecoat pocket and then passed me something. "Use this."

I flicked on the flashlight and we held our breath, waiting for the light to reveal some hidden evil, some specter from the past. We didn't see nothing except cardboard boxes piled in one corner and an old, empty picture frame leaning against the wall.

The floor was lined with boards and I tested one with my foot. "Can we walk on these?"

Liza nodded and clamped her hand on my arm, her fingernails digging into my skin as I took a step forward. I kicked at one of the boxes and it slid to the floor with a crash. Its contents tumbled out. Monopoly, Snakes & Ladders, Yahtzy and some other games.

"For crying out loud," I huffed. "There's nothing here. No voices."

"B-but I heard someone up here," she said. "I swear I did."

"Well, there's those Poker chips you was looking for last month."

Liza swallowed hard. "How'd they get here? I'm never in my attic."

I rolled my eyes at her, thinking that maybe she came up to her attic lots of times. Maybe she just didn't remember. She'd been having a lot of memory lapses lately. Some days I wondered if she was suffering from Old Timers Disease.

"Nothing here," I sighed, patting her on the shoulder.

It was when we were putting the games back in the box that we did find something.

A Ouija board.

"It's eeee-vil," Liza said, refusing to touch it.

I scowled. "Whatcha mean, evil?"

"It's the devil's board game."

When Liza said this, the attic grew colder than the cemetery in the middle of February. I looked down at the Ouija board, then picked it up. It appeared harmless enough. Wasn't too heavy either. I don't know what got into me but all of a sudden I was overcome by curiosity.

"I wanna see it," I said stubbornly.

I took the game downstairs, much to Liza's dismay, and put the box on the scratched coffee table. I turned on a lamp then pulled out the board and set it on the table. Tipping the box, I watched a small piece of wood tumble to the floor.

"What's this for?"

Liza explained how you rest your fingers on the wood and ask the spirits a question. She told me that the spirits would push the piece of wood and spell out the answers on the board. I thought, this I gotta see. But Liza wanted nothing to do with it. So me being a good friend and all promised to make her favorite carrot cake if she played the game with me.

We put our fingers on the wood and stared into each other's eyes.

"What should we ask it?" Liza's voice trembled with fear.

"Who are you, Great Spirit?" I asked in a spooky voice.

I tried hard not to laugh at the horrified expression on my friend's face while we waited for an answer. Nothing happened. I was gonna take my hand off when all of a sudden the piece of wood shot out from beneath my fingers.

N.

"Liza," I scolded. "You pushed it."

My friend shook her head, her face whiter than bleached cotton.

I rested my fingers back on the wood and we waited again. We were mesmerized when it moved across to the A.

NA.

Then it moved to the T. Then the A again.

NATA.

Liza leaned forward. "You think it's Natalie Brown from down the road? You know, the lady who died last Sunday."

I shook my head. "Dunno. Let's ask it another question instead."

Me and my big mouth.

I asked the board if it had a message for us. When we read it, Liza and I gasped. Then we shoved the board into the box and stuffed it under the couch.

You're probably wondering what the Ouija board said.

It said: DEATH BOBBY T.

Bobby Truman was the only Bobby T. we knew. And the very next day, he was hit by a train when his truck stalled in the crossing. He was only eighteen years old when he died.

* * *

The day after that, Liza phoned me and said we had to get rid of the Ouija board. She couldn't have anything that evil in her house. So I met her on the corner and we took the board to the dumpster behind the laundromat and left it there. That was that!

Or so we thought.

Later that night I got a phone call. Liza was histerikle. "Come over, quick!"

When I got to my friend's house, I saw that every light in her house was on.

"What's going on?" I asked when she pushed me into her living room.

And then I saw it.

Right there, in the middle of the coffee table, was the Ouija board.

"Jesus Murphy!" I muttered. "Why'd ya go back and get it?"

Liza swore up and down that she never went back for that board. It had just showed up on her table after suppertime. It still smelled like garbage and laundry soap.

"We have to find out what it wants," I told her. "Then maybe it'll leave you alone."

When we asked, the board came back with...DEATH SERENA U.

Serena Underhill was a girl I taught piano to. She was only 16.

I stared down at the board then said to Liza, "Pack it up."

We left her house just after 8. She was holding a plastic bag with the board in it. She held it out in front with her fingertips as if she was holding fresh dog crap. We walked four blocks down to Ling's Noodle House and shoved the bag into a trashcan just before the garbage truck came. We stood there and watched as all the trash was compacted.

* * *

The next day Serena Underhill drowned in Mears Creek.

And by suppertime the Ouija board was back on Liza's table, reeking of sesame oil.

Now I know what you're thinking. You're thinking that Liza went out and got back that board. I admit it. I was thinking the same thing. So when she called me that night, I went over and got the board. Then I took the bus to the ocean by myself. I walked along the boardwalk on the water's edge and flung that Ouija board out as far as I could. I waited while it was dragged out to sea and I stayed there until I saw that gawddamn board sink into the ocean.

Half an hour later, I got home and found Liza sobbing on my front porch. In her hands she held a sopping wet Ouija board.

Oh my Jesus, and all that's above! I was more than shocked. For the first time in my life I was deathly afraid.

Realizing that we had no choice, we sat at my kitchen table with the board between us.

"What on God's green earth do you want?" I yelled.

My fingers tingled as the wood slowly slid across the board.

U.

I thought of Ursula Bigelow or Ugene Pierce.

The wood stayed where it was.

"U?" Liza moaned. "What does that mean?"

We waited for the board to spell more but the wood didn't move.

Liza bit her lip. "We asked what it wants. I-I think it wants us."

Suddenly the room vibrated and we heard a wicked laugh echo through the house. We snatched back our hands and watched the wood race around the board.

LIZASHAR—

"We gotta get rid of this thing," I said.

"We tried that!" Liza cried. "But it just keeps coming back."

When I glanced at the fireplace in my living room I got an idea. We built us a fire and when it was blazing hot we fed it pieces of the box.

"Put another log on the fire," I sang bitterly, tossing the wood piece into the flames.

Together we threw the Ouija board into the fire and watched as it slowly crumpled on the edges. When it ignited, we let out a sigh of relief. Me and Liza stayed there, arm in arm, watching the letters slowly fry until the board turned to ashes. And then the smell hit us. The stench of rot and decay was awful—like an Easter egg long forgotten after Easter.

That was the night before last.

* * *

Yesterday morning, I found Liza on her front lawn—dead of a broken neck. Beside her lay the Ouija board with one small scorch mark on its edge.

The sky is blood-red over the lake and the air tastes like death.

I have to hurry. I don't think I got much time left. The board said both of us, so I know it's coming for me next. I'm so afraid but I have to try to get rid of this thing one last time and I have to let everyone know the truth. I was the one who opened Pandora's Box. I'm the one who needs to close it.

Just so its clear, Liza and I tried throwing the Ouija board in a dumpster and a trashcan. I threw it in the ocean and when that didn't work, we both watched it burn in the fireplace. Each and every time, the gawdawful evil thing ended up back at Liza's.

Then again, Liza never could throw anything away. A pack rat. That's what she was.

And my best friend.

I'm writing this letter and watching the Ouija board burn. This time I soaked it in lighter fluid, and when it's done burning I'm gonna take the ashes and bury them by the lake.

When we asked it that first night what its name was, we should have waited. Actually, we never should have asked in the first place.

NATA—

I know now that only one other letter was missing and that if I held a mirror to it, the word would read backwards—the devil of all evils.

100

SATAN!

He's coming for me. I can feel it in my bones. It's all my fault. I was curious. And you know what they say about curiosity.

I have to get these ashes to the lake.

Be back later...I hope.

Sharon Kaye

On February 13th, 2004, my aunt Sharon was found lying near Aurora Lake, her gaping eyes frozen in fear and her hands blistered and burnt. The coroner said she drowned. But I think something else killed her—something insidious and older than time.

While packing away my aunt's belongings at her lakeside cottage, I discovered this letter in a box of old party games. Curious, I read the letter and then reached into the box, pulling out something damp and slightly scorched. A OUIJA board.

You know what they say about curiosity...

Caller Unknown

It's not easy being a hired assassin, especially when there are dead bodies to discreetly dispose of and evidence to eliminate. I take pride in my work and I try to do my very best. I offer a money back guarantee. If you aren't happy with the results, neither am I.

I wasn't always an assassin; I used to be a nurse. I promised to do no harm. Whoops. Hospital cutbacks, longer shifts, fewer holidays and a cut in pay pissed me off to no end and I decided to quit. It was either that or I'd have had to kill the head nurse who did the scheduling, and at that time the idea of hurting someone was just that—an idea.

I suppose some might call me a sociopath or psycho or serial killer. I like to look at myself as more of a female Dexter. You know, eliminating the bad elements in the world so the rest of us can live easier, safer. Like Dexter, I have a code. The Becky McFarland code. If you screwed someone, fucked someone over or hurt someone, you're on my list.

The first time I killed someone I was thirty-one, living in Toronto and working in Borealis Gallery. One evening, an older man in a sharp three-piece suit came into the gallery just before closing. I thought he was interested in the art on the wall, when in fact he was more interested in the floor—in getting me on that floor so I could perform *Whistling Dixie* on his dick-see.

"Down on the floor now, bitch," he said, aiming a gun at my head.

I immediately flashed back to when I was a child, when a shadow would enter my room at night and touch me. My stepfather was a bastard with an insatiable appetite. I'd kill him now, but he's already dead. No, I didn't do it. But I sure wanted to. The bastard was lucky. He died from cancer when I was fifteen.

On my stepfather's final day, my mother left me alone with him. I placed my hand over his mouth and nose. I wanted to stop him from exhaling and poisoning the air.

I leaned close and smiled. "I'm so happy you're dying, but can you hurry up already?"

He blinked once and I removed my hand. We had an understanding.

Later, with the stranger in the gallery, I envisioned my stepfather's face in his final moments. I wanted this man to have that same empty look. I didn't want him to continue poisoning my world, so I brushed up against the desk, then carefully sank to my knees.

The man unbuckled his belt and dropped his pants. "Do it and I'll let you live."

I stared up at him and said, "Say you're sorry and I'll let you."

"Let me what?"

"Live."

He laughed, then reached for my head, but before he made contact I withdrew my right hand from behind my back. The scissors gleamed in the soft light and the room suddenly emptied of all sound, all oxygen.

Whoosh!

With only a second's hesitation I stabbed the scissors into his leg. I knew I'd hit a main artery when blood began to spray everywhere. It washed across my face, down my neck and onto the floor, crimson blossoms that bloomed and multiplied.

The man dropped the gun and shrieked in pain. He dropped to the floor and was dead within minutes.

I waited ten more just to be sure. Then I called 911.

"Someone tried to...to...r-rape me," I stuttered to the woman on the other end of the phone. "I had to d-defend myself. I think I k-killed him." I let my sobs flow freely.

Everything happened so quickly after that. While the man's body was sent to the morgue, I was taken to a hospital where I caught sight of my reflection. I saw red. My hands were covered in dried blood. My face looked like a gruesome tribal mask; my tears had cleaned pathways down to my chin. The color of my shirt was red too.

There was a trial, but it was short. The man had attacked three other women in Toronto. I was the only one who'd fought back. Self-defense. People called me a hero, but I knew the truth. I was just a survivor. A survivor who actually enjoyed ridding the world of trash like that man.

So now I'm an assassin. It's a job I'm good at. Hell, in this crappy economy, it's a job—period.

Whenever I meet a potential client, there are no names exchanged. As far as they know, I have no name. I hand out silver-edged business cards that read: *Pest Extermination Services of Toronto. P.E.S.T.* for short. You won't find me in any phone book and the phone number on the card belongs to a throw-away cell phone.

No one knows my name, except you. But you won't tell anyone. Will you? No, I didn't think so.

If you're unfortunate enough to be on the receiving end of my services, I send you to Mc-FAR-Land and believe me, there's no clown with orange hair waiting to greet you.

I officially started my profession when my friend Carla was attacked in the park one night. She wasn't raped, but she was beaten to a messy pulp. I would've missed her if she'd died. I don't say that about just anyone.

Weeks after the attack, Carla swore she was being stalked.

"They never caught him," she'd told me, her eyes filled with panic. "Becky, I know he's the one leaving me breathy messages on my answering machine."

Breathy, as in that's all he did. Like old campy horror flicks, he'd call, breathe heavy and hang up. Caller ID brought up "caller unknown".

One night she called me. "Can you come over?"

"What's wrong?"

"I think he's outside my apartment, across the street."

"Did he call you?"

There was a sniffle on the other end. "Yes, and I'm scared silly."

At first I thought she might be imagining things. Then I realized something. What if she wasn't?

"Becky, if you come over and keep me company, I'll pay you $100."

I let out a sigh. "I'll be over in ten minutes. Until I get there, don't answer the phone and keep—"

"The door locked," she finished.

I hung up and left for my divine intervention with Carla's stalker.

"I'm so glad you're here," she whispered when I arrived.

"Why are you whispering? He's not here."

"He's standing near the newspaper box on the corner." She pointed toward her living room window. "Go see. He's wearing a long black trench coat."

I quickly moved to the window and stood to one side. With my index finger, I hooked the drape aside and peeked out into the night. The view from the second floor was clear as day. The lamp on the street corner lit up the target, even better than if I'd painted a bulls-eye on him.

"You sure it's him?" I asked.

"See the silver buckles on his boots? I recognize them."

I took another look. Sure enough, something sparkled on his boots.

104

"No decent man would be caught dead wearing boots like that," Carla muttered.

But an indecent one would, I thought.

I studied my friend closely. "You don't look well."

Carla still carried the bruises from the attack and she was shaking and sweating. Her hands were clenched so tightly they looked like they'd implode. Her eyes had bags beneath them that were so big and puffy they could store change. In fact, she was barely recognizable.

"You haven't been sleeping, have you, Carla?"

She shook her head.

"Have you been eating?"

"A bit, but nothing stays down."

My decision was made. Something had to be done.

"This man attacked you. And now he's trying to intimidate you. He's not done with you."

"I know. What should I do, Becky? I'm terrified."

I grabbed her jacket and was out the door before she could stop me. I took the stairs to the back exit and strode across the driveway to my car. Lifting the trunk, I rummaged around until I found the perfect accompaniment. A tire iron.

"Okay, you bastard, let's see how *you* like it."

I maneuvered around the building and strolled down the street.

Silver Buckles took the bait.

I headed for the park, ducked into some bushes and waited.

I didn't have to wait long.

There you are. Come to Mama.

Silver Buckles hesitated.

It was the longest minute of my life. And the *last* minute of his.

I crept up behind him and swung the tire iron. I felt his scull give way under pressure as the weapon in my hand made contact with the back of his head, the hooked end embedding itself into his scalp like a parasitic tick.

'COD is blunt force trauma to the brain,' I imagined the coroner saying.

Silver Buckles fell to the ground with barely a groan. Blood and brain matter oozed from beneath his hair and when I pulled the tire iron away, a patch of his scalp came with it. His eyes fluttered as he stared up at me, a puzzled expression on his bloodied face.

"Who are you?" he rasped.

"I'm the last person you'll see before Satan takes you."

Less than a minute later, Silver Buckles took his last breath.

I rolled him in a tarp from the house next door. It was undergoing renovations. Then I dumped the body in the trunk of a car I *borrowed*. It had been parked, unlocked, a block from Carla's house. Someone had conveniently left the keys tucked into the visor.

I drove to a private dock, found a dingy and rowed Silver Buckles out into the bay. I rolled him over the side and watched him sink below the surface. Then I drove home and called Carla.

In a breathy voice I said, "He's gone." Then I hung up.

That was the day I became what I am today. Guardian to the abused and purveyor of evil souls to the devil. My code was born from the moment I killed him. I became an assassin for hire, the 'caller unknown' who leaves a breathy message when the job is done.

Now I have a new job.

I'm coming for *you*.

You know what you've done.

Skeletons in the Closet

Many families have secrets. Shameful events formed from deception, humiliation or guilt. Some have buried their secrets where no one will ever find them. Some have spun a web of lies so convincing that even they start to believe them. Others hold onto their shame and wrap themselves in it, like a protective fur coat. Every family has "skeletons in the closet", and I was about to unearth mine.

On this auspicious spring evening, I had parked my car in front of the behemoth grand manor that had been the family home for four generations. The house sat regally atop Hallowed Hill, just four miles north of the city. It was constructed from dull gray brick and small windows. Overall, a cold, dreary welcome. Even the thunderous skies that boiled overhead seemed to be warning me away. I turned deaf ears to it. Maybe I should've listened.

I used the key Grammy had given me and the front door squealed in rebellion. I entered the family home with a sense of excitement that wouldn't last long.

"Some doors are never meant to be opened."

I wish I had listened to Grammy's wise words, but the self-assured adult I had become shrugged off the advice. Funny how we think we know better than those who have lived far longer and seen much more.

After a quick tour of the lower floor, I was satisfied to see that everything was in its place, exactly as I remembered it. Pausing at the bottom of the stairs, I sighed. My eyes were drawn to the upper landing. For a minute I thought I saw someone crouched near the rails.

"Hello?" My voice echoed through cavernous walls. "Is anyone here?"

No reply.

Laughing at my paranoia, I headed upstairs and followed the hall to the room at the end. Grammy's room. I reached out and a visible spark

107

flew from the shiny metal knob to my fingertips. I jumped back, startled and slightly breathless.

"Jesus!" I covered my mouth with one hand.

"Don't take the Lord's name in vain, Emma." I could hear Grammy's voice so clearly in my mind it was like she was standing right behind me.

My eyes darted guiltily down the hall. There was no one around, no one to hear my slip. But one could never be too careful.

"Sorry," I said, feeling like a child again.

I looked at the antique keys on the tarnished silver key ring in my hand. Grammy had given me the keys at the hospital. She'd told me to go check out my inheritance. Told me to stay out of her bedroom closet. Just like she had so many years ago when I had visited her in the house at the top of Hallowed Hill. A house that I had once sworn was haunted.

"Emma..."

I jumped, certain I'd heard the deep voice of my grandfather, the one I recalled from my youth. His voice made me think of lollipops and pony rides. That's how I remembered him. How I *wanted* to remember him.

Grampy had been a war hero. When I was about six, he'd sat me on his knee and told me how he'd rescued his buddies in Vietnam after their chopper was shot down by enemy troops. Grampy had flown in, dangling on a line suspended over the heads of the Vietcong, all the while dodging bullets and machine gun spray.

Whenever I thought of Grampy, I pictured him hanging in the air. Suspended.

When he'd returned home, he wasn't the same man. That's what Grammy always told my mother. He started drinking and fighting with other war vets in bars. He'd also broken bones and bloodied noses of those who were against the war. Grammy said he always walked headfirst into a fight, with his big mouth flapping and his fists up and ready.

I'd never seen that part of him. Only the aftermath.

Too many times, my mother had gone out in the middle of the night to pick him up, half-carrying him inside. I woke up on these nights, troubled by Grampy's loud slurring and my mother's chastising anger. When I saw Grampy the next morning, he always smiled at me and called me his "Punkin". He'd take me out back where I'd watch him polish and repair one of his old cars, while I handed him the tools. We were both covered in grease by the time he was done.

Grampy was my hero.

Until he disappeared a week before Christmas. I was eighteen. He left my poor Grammy heartbroken, my mother without a father and me without my favorite person in the whole world. That's when I started resenting him. I couldn't help it.

"Emma..."

There was a cool draft in the hall and I blamed it for my imagination running wild. The house was empty. Except for me.

Wasn't it?

I turned the knob and stepped into my grandmother's room.

The master bedroom appeared to be never-ending, a series of three rooms connected by wide archways and stone pillars. This room was a mystery to me as I'd never been allowed inside whenever I'd visited. It had been Grammy's private sanctuary. Still was.

"Grammy?" I whispered. I almost expected her to answer.

I entered and flipped on the light. A warm golden glow shone down on me as I stepped into the floral sitting room, which held a mahogany bookshelf, a flower-patterned sofa and matching high-back chair with ornately carved arms and padded rests. There were tables of all sizes and heights, stained in shades of warm oak and many adorned with crystal bowls and vases. Grammy had once told me that Grampy had brought back much of the wood furniture and crystal from places like Italy, Germany and England.

I passed through the archway at the opposite end and entered Grammy's bedroom. A canopy bed sat regally on a raised platform in the middle of the room. The ceiling in this section was about fifteen feet high, with elaborate crown molding and inset ceiling tiles from Italy. A pathway covered in thick, lush carpets completely framed the floor around the bed.

I followed the carpet path, admiring numerous pieces of furniture and artwork that I suspected were originals and valuable, but it was the bed that really intrigued me. Larger than any other I'd ever seen, it seemed fit for a king.

Or a queen.

Elegantly draped fabrics in gold and crimson tones hung from carved posts and swayed from one top corner to the next. Embroidered bedding in matching tones covered the bed, and I stared at it, wondering what it must be like to sleep in such luxury.

I resisted the urge to throw myself onto the bed. It wasn't easy.

The scent of perfume lingered in the air. Chanel No. 5. Grammy's favorite. Every Christmas since the late 1930s, Grampy would buy her a new bottle.

Grammy's warning in the hospital came back to me.

"Stay out of my closet, Emma."

I glanced at the closet door. It was plain and uninteresting, no etching, no fancy design, just solid wood, iron hinges and a lever handle instead of a doorknob. I shrugged, wondering why Grammy had been so adamant about me not going in her closet. What was the big deal?

"Maybe that's where she's hiding her stash of medicinal marijuana," I muttered, though I doubted she'd ever tried the stuff.

I let my fingers drift over the surface of the furniture as I strolled around the room. I left a clean trail in the dust on the surface of everything I touched.

The colonial oak dresser at the far end of the room displayed various family photographs. I picked up a photo of Grammy and my mother, when she was a teenager. They both looked happy and carefree. I put it back, my attention drawn to a baby picture. Me, when I was two. I was a chubby baby, with squinty eyes, sausage links for arms and legs and three chins. Scowling, I set the photo down on the dresser, backwards. The other photographs revealed family members I couldn't identify. There wasn't one picture of Grampy.

I looked at the closet door again. Was it open a crack?

I approached it, telling myself I'd make sure it was closed, just as Grammy wanted. When I'd seen her in the hospital, she told me she'd made arrangements for someone to pack up all her personal belongings, including whatever was in the closet.

"When that's done," she'd said, "you can do whatever you want with the room. With the whole house. It's yours."

I reached for the handle and opened the door.

The design of Grammy's bedroom closet was early walk-in style. Extra wide, extra deep and very dark. I reached for the light switch and flicked it on. The light bulb flickered and hissed. Then it died.

I was thrown into partial darkness, the light from the bedroom casting a pale slice about halfway inside. The far end of the closet was submerged in shadows.

I sniffed and scowled. A musty smell lingered in the air.

"You could use some Febreeze in here, Grammy."

I took in the colorful clothing that lined one wall of the closet. Grammy had her own flamboyant style. Wearing flowing jackets, caftans, silks from China and India, all in bright colors and patterns, she liked to stand out in a crowd.

On a shelf above the clothing were six mannequin heads with various colored wigs, from blond to auburn. They were remnants of Grammy's battle with cancer—one she'd beaten with finesse.

I fingered the shoulder length blond wig. It reminded me of my mother, whom I hadn't seen in a while. She'd taken off on an around-the-

110

world tour. She sometimes sent me postcards from one exotic place or another.

"Why did you leave me here all alone, Mom?" I asked the mannequin head. "Why did you make me responsible for Grammy?"

I resented my mother. But I loved her too. Sometimes when I thought of her, I missed her so badly I wanted to curl up and cry my heart out.

I took a few steps into the shadows. Somewhere over here was the old trunk that Grammy was adamant about moving to her new home. Another step into the dark brought me up against the trunk. I wondered how heavy it was.

Before I changed my mind, I yanked on the corner of the trunk and was surprised to find it moved quite easily. Sliding my hands around it, I discovered handles on both sides. The trunk was too wide for me to carry, so I dragged it across the floor until it caught on a floorboard. I heard a soft cracking sound and gave another sharp pull.

The trunk slid into the light.

There was a large keyhole on the front. Was it locked?

I pushed the lid. It didn't budge. I tried all the keys on the key ring. Nothing.

Peering over one shoulder, I examined the room.

Where would Grammy hide the key?

Her dresser beckoned me. There were three drawers down each side and two cupboard doors in the middle. I opened each drawer and felt around underneath Grammy's clothes. It was a bit uncomfortable searching through her undergarments, especially when I came up empty. I opened the doors. Two shelves of sweaters. Nothing else.

I was about to walk away, when I noticed a small groove on the strip of wood that ran above the cupboard shelf, just under the dresser top. I hooked my fingers in the groove and tugged. A hidden drawer slid out.

And there it was. The key.

"I just know you're the right one," I murmured.

Walking back to the trunk, I pushed the key in the lock and turned it. There was a quiet click. The lid popped open a quarter of an inch.

"Okay, Grammy," I said, exhaling. "Let's see what you've got in here that's so important."

Papers. The trunk was filled with all kinds of papers. Envelopes, some old and some unused. Stacks of letters bound by elastic bands. A pile of photographs and a small box, which when opened revealed postcards.

Probably from my mother.

111

A black leather folder caught my eye. My name was on it.

"Looks like I've got some reading to do."

I grabbed the folder. As an afterthought, I took a stack of letters and the box. Placing these on the bed, I decided I'd spend the night reading.

Okay, I was snooping. But she was my grandmother after all.

An uncomfortable feeling swept over me. I was invading my grandmother's privacy. Logically, I knew I should put everything back and forget about it. But something illogical urged me on.

I plumped up the pillows on Grammy's bed, turned on the lamp and settled into the softness of duvets and feathers. I placed the box in my lap, opened it and splayed out a handful of postcards. Photos of familiar and unfamiliar worldwide landmarks greeted me. Paris, Italy, Germany, Spain…the destinations were varied.

"Definitely from my Mom." I gritted my teeth. "So let's see what she had to say to you, Grammy."

I turned over a postcard. It was blank. Frowning, I turned over another. Blank too. I flipped over the pile in my hands and fanned them. Not a word or signature on any of them.

It didn't make sense.

I dropped the cards back in the box and reached for the letters. Removing the elastic band, I examined the top envelope. It was addressed to Marilyn Ingram, my grandmother. The sender was R.V.P.H., with an address about five miles out of the city. A charity perhaps?

I opened the letter, dated in December of the previous year.

Dear Mrs. Ingram, the letter stated. *I hope this Christmas season finds you well. With regards to the resident, she has been showing signs of severe emotional distress, just as we predicted. This seems to be the most stressful time of year for her, and so we'd advise against your monthly visit. However, if you do decide to come by, please be aware that we've had to adjust her medication so she may not be fully alert or even aware of your visit. Also, please note that she still insists that she's traveling through Europe and is unaware of her actual surroundings. At this time, we cannot recommend her release.*

I stared at the letter. "What the hell?"

The word *resident* jumped out at me. And the word *medication*.

"*She still insists that she's traveling through Europe,*" I read aloud.

Oh. My. God. My mother was insane.

I ripped another letter from the stack. The date was January 15, 2010.

Dear Mrs. Ingram, the resident is still unaware of her situation and she insists she's visiting Scotland. The staff feels confident that she will

112

regain both her memory and her sanity. She did appear less confused after your last visit. We look forward to seeing you again.

I swallowed hard and tasted bile. Blinking back tears, I stared at the envelope. *R.V.P.H.* was some kind of Psychiatric Hospital.

I flipped through the envelopes, reading the postmarks. They dated back to March of 2005.

With my heart pounding, I strode to the trunk and removed the other letters. Again, I checked the postmarks. These dated back to 2001, the year Grampy had disappeared. Was there a connection?

Something sparkled on the floor of the closet.

Thinking Grammy had dropped a piece of jewelry, I entered and crouched low, my hand grazing the rough wood floor. "Ouch!"

A splinter stuck me on my palm. I plucked it out and sucked at the wound. Then I caught sight of the sparkle again. Something had fallen into a hole in the floorboard, a hole I'd created when I'd dragged the trunk across the floor.

I tried prying the board with my fingers, but I wasn't strong enough.

"Hammer," I muttered. I'd seen one earlier, under the bathroom sink.

Returning from the bathroom with hammer in hand, I used the clawed end to pry up the loose corner of the board. The overpowering scent of mothballs made my eyes water. Coughing, I wiped my eyes and continued working on the board. A few minutes of prying resulted in success, but before I could lift it, I heard a door slam downstairs.

"Emma?"

It was Grammy.

A surge of red hot heat flared through my cheeks.

What was I doing? Not only had I disobeyed Grammy's request to not open the closet, I'd read her personal letters, ones that weren't meant for my eyes, and now I was ripping up her floor.

Guilt rebelled against resentment.

How could Grammy keep this from me? How could she hide what my mother was? A nutcase in some psycho hospital. What right did Grammy have to keep that from me?

Footsteps sounded on the stairs.

Shit! I had to put the trunk back. And the letters.

With my heart racing, I tossed the letters in the trunk, along with the box of postcards. I dragged the trunk into the closet.

"Emma? Are you in here?"

Wiping a dusty hand against my brow, I emerged from the closet, only to be confronted by my grandmother. Her snow white hair was pinned into a bun, accentuating her gaunt appearance. Wire-rimmed glasses had slid halfway down her matriarchal nose and she pushed them up with a boney finger. She puckered her lips, reprimanding me wordlessly from a distance.

In her hand was the black leather folder I'd left on the bed.

"You shouldn't be poking around in someone else's belongings," she said, resting heavily against her cane. She frowned. "You scratched the floor."

I didn't know what to say. Two fresh gouge marks marred the hardwood floor, disappearing into the closet.

"We need to talk, Emma." She held up the folder. "Did you peek?"

I shook my head and held my stance as she squinted at me and tried to determine if I was lying.

"Let's make a pot of tea," Grammy said in a tired voice.

In her world, a pot of tea was the solution for everything.

I followed her down the stairs, pausing with her as she caught her breath every so often. A million questions swarmed through my brain, and I wanted to bat them away. I knew that once I'd opened Pandora's Box and asked those questions there would be no turning back. No more living in denial.

Grammy puttered around the kitchen, filling a tarnished kettle with water and setting it on the gas stove. She set two tea cups and saucers on the small table in the corner, then gathered a silver serving tray with cream, sugar and two spoons.

She waved me over as the kettle whistled. "Have a seat, dear."

I sat down across from her.

She placed the folder on the table, centering it between us like a barrier. Then she ignored it and went about preparing the tea. "You still like yours weak?"

"Yes, Grammy."

She poured my tea and waited her usual three minutes before pouring her own. I silently added a dose of cream and a spoon of sugar to my cup. I needed all the fortitude I could get.

"Did you snoop through anything else in my trunk?" she asked.

"I didn't snoop—" I caught myself in the lie. "Okay, sorry, I did. I found the letters and the postcard."

Grammy blinked a few times and turned away. When she spoke, her voice was strained. "Did you read them?"

"Yes." I took a sip of the tea. It scalded my tongue.

"So you know…"

"That my mother is a nutcase?"

Grammy's head shot up. "Don't say that."

114

"I *know*, Grammy. I know that my mother isn't traveling around the world, living her easy breezy carefree lifestyle. She's locked up in some hospital because she's crazy. With a capital *C*."

"Emma!" A tear rolled down Grammy's cheek.

"You don't have to pretend anymore. I can handle it."

"Can you?"

"I'm not a child. I can handle the truth."

Grammy leaned forward and placed a frail hand on the folder. "If it's truth you want, it's all in here. But I have to warn you, you won't like what you find." She hitched in a breath and wiped her eyes. "It's not what you think, Emma."

"Nothing's what I think anymore, is it?"

Grammy slumped in the chair, her shoulders deflating. "No, it isn't."

"What I don't get is why you waited so long to tell me."

"They told me to wait. Until you started asking questions."

"Who told you?"

"The doctors."

I allowed this to sink in. My mother's doctors knew she had a child, but thought it better to wait to let me in on the big secret until I started wondering what the heck was going on. Nice doctors.

I reached for the folder and for a moment I wasn't sure Grammy would release it. But she did. Begrudgingly.

"After you've read that," Grammy said, "I know you'll have questions. I can stay here—"

"No." When I realized how ungrateful that sounded, I softened my voice. "I'm sorry, Grammy. I'm really tired. I'll read it in the morning and call you right after."

"Are you sure, dear?"

I nodded, part of me wondering whether I was making a mistake in letting her go before I'd learned the whole truth. *And nothing but the truth, so help me God.*

When we were finished our tea, I escorted Grammy to the door.

"Make sure you call me tomorrow morning," she said, "as soon as you read it."

"I will. I promise."

I watched her walk down the sidewalk to the awaiting taxi. Once the taillights faded, I closed the front door and rested my back against it. Exhaustion had set in. I felt it in my bones and even my teeth. My body ached to curl up on a soft mattress and sleep. But my mind was all chatter.

What's the scoop on my mother? How crazy is she? What will I find in that folder? Don't I want to look now? Why wait until morning? Go on, read it now.

I grabbed my head with both hands. "Shut up!"

I returned to the kitchen and approached the table. The folder lay there so innocently. Papers and words. That's all it was.

And truth.

"If it's truth you want, it's all in here," Grammy had said.

"I want the truth," I said to the empty room.

I sat down. I inched my fingers toward the folder. When I touched it, it seemed hot.

You're imagining things.

Though I'd told Grammy I'd read the documents in the morning, there was no way I could wait that long. I had to read them now. I had to know.

I opened the folder, drew out the first page and read it. Then I read the next sheet. And the next. With each page, my confusion grew. Terror set in.

Oh my God.

I read every page twice, pinching myself occasionally to make sure I wasn't dreaming. This was real. This was the truth.

I stood up, my legs trembling. Even my hands shook. Leaving the folder open on the table, I wandered into the den. I needed something stronger than tea and I knew where Grammy kept the good stuff. Her bourbon collection was the talk of the town.

Two glasses later, I felt calmer. I brought a third glass into the kitchen and stared at the file, willing it to burst into flames. I considered destroying it, but I suspected there were other copies.

I picked up the final page and read it once more, allowing every word to sink in. I was desperate to remember my mother's face. That last day. The day when tragedy had struck…

A glimmer of a memory surfaced and I hissed in a breath. My mother had gone out late that night to bring Grampy home after one of his late night binges at the local bar. When they'd returned, they'd woken the entire house. I remembered the loud voices and vicious words. They scared me.

I massaged my forehead, struggling to recall what had happened next.

I'd gotten out of bed and was heading down the upper hallway when I heard my Grampy roar. It was the one sound that made everyone nervous.

Though I was eighteen years old at the time, fear reduced me to a quivering child. I crept to the landing and peeked over the rail. Grampy and my mother were fighting, pushing each other. He was trying to leave the house again and my mother wouldn't let him. He smacked her hard against the face. I sucked in a shocked breath. My hero was beating on my mother.

My mother hit him back. A few feet away, Grammy cowered against the wall, trembling with fear. "Stop it, Walter! Leave her alone. She's just trying to help you."

"I don't need her help," Grampy roared, his fists lashing out at my mother.

Terrified, I sobbed on the landing above them. My head felt like someone had taken a jackhammer to it. Panic robbed me of breath and my vision grew blurry.

Now as I recalled this fateful night, my head started to hammer.

The scene in my mind switched. I saw Grampy. Lying on the floor. Soaked in blood. Unmoving.

Dead.

"Oh, Jesus," I whispered. "It can't be true."

The vision grew more defined and I saw my grandfather's pocket watch. It lay next to him, also covered in blood.

The vision faded and I stared up at the landing, picturing a scared teen, her face between the rails, watching the violence below.

I plodded up the stairs.

Entering Grammy's bedroom, I went to the closet and yanked the trunk along the floor, anger surging within me. Again, the trunk caught on the loose floorboard and it cracked and lifted.

The glimmer drew me closer.

Crawling on my knees, I waved at the cloying scent of mothballs and ripped up the remainder of the board. I tossed it aside. The space beneath was large, and it wasn't empty. My grandfather's pocket watch rested on top of a four foot wide blanketed shroud. The shroud, about six feet in length, was surrounded by mothballs.

I picked up the watch and stared at the shroud.

Grampy hadn't left my grandmother for another woman. He hadn't left Grammy at all.

"Grammy, what did you do?"

"I did what I had to, Emma."

I turned.

Grammy stood in the doorway, tears pouring down her cheeks. "I couldn't leave you tonight. I knew you'd never wait until morning to read the reports."

"I'm starting to remember."

"I figured you would one day."

I flicked a look at the shroud beneath the floorboards. I knew what it was. *Who* it was. With gentle moves, I pealed back the blanket, carefully pulling it away from the skeletons that rested within its cocoon.

Grampy and my mother. She was wrapped lovingly in his arms.

They looked peaceful.

"He killed my mother," I sobbed.

"I tried to stop him," Grammy said, hobbling over to me.

I reached for her, hugging her tightly. "I know. But he was drunk. He didn't know what he was doing. She was dead before she hit the floor at the bottom of the stairs."

"I thought you'd die too," Grammy said, gulping in breaths of strained air.

"I didn't mean it."

"I know, dear." She stroked my hair. "It was an accident."

Grasping her hand, I led her to the bed and we sat down as the past washed over us, all of its terror and guilt finally setting us free.

I reached in my pocket and pulled out the last page from the folder.

"When I found the letters and the postcards, I thought I'd figured things out," I told her.

"I did what I had to do to keep you safe. I didn't want you taken from me too." Grammy took a deep breath. "I wrote the letters that were supposed to be from your mother because the doctors thought it best. At least until you started remembering."

"But it took so long."

"I know. Sometimes I thought you'd never remember. Then I could take this to my grave. All of it."

"Grampy pushed my mother down the stairs."

My heart was heavy with the burden of truth.

"I didn't even know you were awake," Grammy said quietly. "I saw you charge at him when he reached the top."

"And I pushed him down the stairs," I said, shaking my head slowly.

"You were upset that he'd hurt your mother. It was an accident, dear."

I gazed into her eyes. "You hid their bodies. Lied about where they were. To everyone. Even my doctors."

Grammy looked away. "I'm not proud of that. I wanted to tell your doctors the truth. In the end, I didn't have to. You refused to speak to anyone. Refused to eat." She took my hands and kissed them. "I had no choice, Emma. To keep you safe—to help you—I had to lie to them and hide the truth. I didn't realize the damage I'd done until it was too late."

I watched her, knowing that in her heart she thought she'd made the best decision. I knew that her choice was dependent on two factors. She feared what would happen to me if my guilt were to be known and she was deathly afraid of being alone.

I thought back to earlier in the week. I hadn't gone to see Grammy in the hospital, like my deluded mind had led me to believe. She'd come to check me out and bring me home. *I* was the patient. Every paper in the folder had *my* name on it, not my mother's. I'd been a resident of River Valley Psychiatric Hospital for the past nine years.

Everything shifted into place, like the magical brick wall from Harry Potter. Like a hazy fog being lifted from my eyes. What was once a fantasy world was now a reality far different than.

"I'll make arrangements to have them buried," Grammy said, interrupting my thoughts. "Private arrangements. No one besides us needs to know what happened. I'll take care of everything."

I nodded. As I watched her make a phone call, I thought of how good Grammy was at taking care of things. She'd looked after me for nine years.

Now it was time for me to take care of her.

"I love you, Grammy."

"I love you too, dear."

Yes, many families have "skeletons in the closet", and on this day I learned that mine was one of them. Literally.

~*~

If you enjoyed this book, please consider writing a short review and posting it on Amazon, Goodreads and/or Barnes and Noble. Reviews are very helpful to other readers and are greatly appreciated by authors, especially me. When you post a review, drop me an email and let me know and I may feature part of it on my blog/site. Thank you. ~ Cheryl

cherylktardif@shaw.ca

Acknowledgements

I wish to thank my dear friend and a very talented author, Betty Dravis, for all her support and encouragement, but mostly for her friendship. Betty, you're a beautiful and gracious lady.

Thank you also to Stephen King for being my idol all through my younger writing years. Thank you for all the nightmares, chills, goose bumps and sleepless nights where I hid under my blankets with a flashlight just so I could finish your books. I've never looked at a storm drain the same since.

To my good friend, author Carol D. O'Dell, whose wise words kept me strong in the face of adversity and who is my comrade against the odds, many thanks. We will succeed!

And to my family and friends, for all your support. Thank you!

* * *

Previously published works:

OUIJA first published in *Silver Moon Magazine*; 2004
Atrophy first published in Silver Moon Magazine; 2005
Picture Perfect first published as an Amazon Short; 2006
A Grave Error first published as an Amazon Short, 2006
Remote Control - first published as a novelette in July 2010; finalist in 2008 Textnovel Contest

KEEP READING! BONUS CONTENT AHEAD!

Reviews

SKELETONS IN THE CLOSET & OTHER CREEPY STORIES

"Tonight I read Cheryl's SKELETONS IN THE CLOSET. My hands turned to ice, my blood ran cold, and my body shook with the shivers. Cheryl writes scary stories." —Eileen Schuh, author of *Schrodinger's Cat*

"Cheryl Kaye Tardif had me gasping with fright...many times over. These stories are shocking! Frightening! Original!" —Betty Dravis, author of *Dream Reachers*

"A thoroughly entertaining and unabashedly Canadian collection of horror shorts - a straightforward, in-your-face, goosebump raising, skin crawling creep fest with brilliantly conceived endings..." —Paul Weiss, Top 1000 Amazon Reviewer

"If you like Stephen King's quirky short stories or are a fan of the Twilight Zone, you will enjoy 'Skeletons in the Closet.'" —John Zur

CHILDREN OF THE FOG

"A chilling and tense journey into every parent's deepest fear." —Scott Nicholson, *The Red Church*

"A nightmarish thriller with a ghostly twist, CHILDREN OF THE FOG will keep you awake...and turning pages!" —Amanda Stevens, author of *The Restorer*

"Reminiscent of *The Lovely Bones*, Cheryl Kaye Tardif weaves a tale of terror that will have you rushing to check on your children as they sleep. With exquisite prose, *Children of the Fog* captures you the moment you begin and doesn't let go until the very end." —bestselling author Danielle Q. Lee, author of *Inhuman*

"Ripe with engaging twists and turns reminiscent of the work of James Patterson, Tardif once again tugs at the most inflexible of heartstrings...*Children of the Fog* possesses you from the touching beginning through to the riveting climax." —Kelly Komm, author of *Sacrifice*, an award-winning fantasy

THE RIVER

"Cheryl Kaye Tardif has once again captivated readers in her third novel and latest suspense thriller, *The River*. Set in the wilds of Canada's north, *The River* combines intrigue, science, love and adventure and is sure to keep readers clamoring for more." —*Edmonton Sun*

"Exciting and vivid...A thrilling adventure where science sniffs harder, desperate to find the fountain-of-youth." —*Midwest Book Review*

DIVINE INTERVENTION

"An exciting book from start to finish. The futuristic elements are believable...plenty of surprising twists and turns. Good writing, good book! Sci-fi and mystery fans will love this book." —*Writer's Digest*

"[An] excellent suspenseful thriller...promises to keep readers engrossed...Watch for more from this gem in the literary world..." —*Real Estate Weekly*

"Believable characters, and scorching plot twists. Anyone who is a fan of J.D. Robb [aka Nora Roberts] will thoroughly enjoy this one...*Divine Intervention* will undeniably leave you smoldering, and dying for more." —Kelly Komm, author of *Sacrifice*, an award-winning fantasy

WHALE SONG

"Tardif's story has that perennially crowd-pleasing combination of sweet and sad that so often propels popular commercial fiction...Tardif, already a big hit in Canada...a name to reckon with south of the border." —*Booklist*

"*Whale Song* is deep and true, a compelling story of love and family and the mysteries of the human heart...a beautiful, haunting novel." —NY Times bestselling novelist Luanne Rice, author of Beach Girls

"A wonderfully well-written novel. Wonderful characters [that] shine. The settings are exquisitely described. The writing is lyrical. *Whale Song* would make a wonderful movie." —*Writer's Digest*

Praise for Cherish D'Angelo (aka Cheryl Kaye Tardif)

LANCELOT'S LADY

"Romance, mystery, danger, black-mail, and twists and surprises, this tale contains them all... Despicable intentions threaten every character in this finely crafted tale of sweet tension...Lancelot's Lady is a non-stop adventure combined with the agonizing struggle to not give in to the magnetism between them. Enticing. Fun." —*Midwest Book Review*

"From the cold rocky shores of Maine to the extravagant mansions of Miami to a lush tropical island in the Bahamas, Cherish D'Angelo takes her heroine through a series of breathtaking romantic adventures that mirror the settings, often in surprisingly ironic ways. A page turner in the best possible sense." —Gail Bowen, author of the award-winning Joanne Kilbourn series

"Cherish D'Angelo has got that mythical "voice" down to a fine art." —Jennifer L. Hart, author of *River Rats*

"*Lancelot's Lady* is riveting. It holds on and won't let you go! Cherish D'Angelo's descriptive powers are amazing. She summons up scenes like genies from bottles!" —Susan J. McLeod, author of *Soul and Shadow*

Now here's a sneak peek of the highly anticipated supernatural thriller,

Children of the Fog

prologue

May 14th, 2007

She was ready to die.

She sat at the kitchen table, a half empty bottle of Philip's precious red wine in one hand, a loaded gun in the other. Staring at the foreign chunk of metal, she willed it to vanish. But it didn't.

Sadie checked the gun and noted the single bullet.

"One's all you need."

If she did it right.

She placed the gun on the table and glanced at a pewter-framed photograph that hung off-kilter above the mantle of the fireplace. It was illuminated by a vanilla-scented candle, one of many that threw flickering shadows over the rough wood walls of the log cabin.

Sam's sweet face stared back at her, smiling.

Alive.

From where she sat, she could see the small chip in his right front tooth, the result of an impatient father raising the training wheels too early. But there was no point in blaming Philip—not when they'd both lost so much.

Not when it's all my fault.

Her gaze swept over the mantle. There were three objects on it besides the candle. Two envelopes, one addressed to Leah and one to Philip, and the portfolio case that contained the illustrations and manuscript on disc for Sam's book.

She had finished it, just like she had promised.

"And promises can't be broken. Right, Sam?"

A single tear burned a path down her cheek.

Sam was gone.

What reason do I have for living now?

She gulped back the last pungent mouthful of Cabernet and dropped the empty bottle. It rolled under the chair, unbroken, rocking on the hardwood floor. Then all was silent, except the antique grandfather clock in the far corner. Its ticking reminded her of the clown's shoe. The one with the tack in it.

Tick, tick, tick...

The clock belched out an ominous gong.

It was almost midnight.

Almost time.

She drew an infinity symbol in the dust on the table.

"Sadie and Sam. For all eternity."

Gong...

She swallowed hard as tears flooded her eyes. "I'm sorry I couldn't save you, baby. I tried to. God, I tried. Forgive me, Sam." Her words ended in a gut-wrenching moan.

Something scraped the window beside her.

She pressed her face to the frosted glass, then jerked back with a gasp. "Go away!"

They stood motionless—six children that drifted from the swirling miasma of night air, haunting her nights and every waking moment. Surrounded by the moonlit fog, they began to chant. *"One fine day, in the middle of the night..."*

"You're not real," she whispered.

"Two dead boys got up to fight."

A small, pale hand splayed against the exterior of the window. Below it, droplets of condensation slid like tears down the glass.

She reached out, matching her hand to the child's. Shivering, she pulled away. "You don't exist."

The clock continued its morbid countdown.

As the alcohol and drug potpourri kicked in, the room began to spin and her stomach heaved. She inhaled deeply. She couldn't afford to get sick. Sam was waiting for her.

Tears spilled down her cheeks. "I'm ready."

Gong...

Without hesitation, she raised the gun to her temple.

"Don't!" the children shrieked.

She pressed the gun against her flesh. The tip of the barrel was cold. Like her hands, her feet...her heart.

A sob erupted from the back of her throat.

The clock let out a final gong. Then it was deathly silent.

It was midnight.

Her eyes found Sam's face again.

"Happy Mother's Day, Sadie."

She took a steadying breath, pushed the gun hard against her skin and clamped her eyes shut.

"Mommy's coming, Sam."

She squeezed the trigger.

1

March 30th, 2007

Sadie O'Connell let out a snicker as she stared at the price tag on the toy in her hand. "What did they stuff this with, laundered money?" She tossed the bunny back into the bin and turned to the tall, leggy woman beside her. "What are you getting Sam for his birthday?"

Her best friend gave her a cocky grin. "What *should* I get him? Your kid's got everything already."

"Don't even go there, my friend."

But Leah was right. Sadie and Philip spoiled Sam silly. Why shouldn't they? They had waited a long time for a baby. Or at least, *she* had. After two miscarriages, Sam's birth had been nothing short of a miracle. A miracle that deserved to be spoiled.

Leah groaned loudly. "Christ, it's a goddamn zoo in here."

Toyz & Twirlz in West Edmonton Mall was crawling with overzealous customers. The first major sale of the spring season always brought people out in droves. Frazzled parents swarmed the toy store, swatting their wayward brood occasionally—the way you'd swat a pesky yellowjacket at a barbecue. One distressed father hunted the aisles for his son, who had apparently taken off on him as soon as his back was turned. In every aisle, parents shouted at their kids, threatening, cajoling, pleading and then predictably giving in.

"So who let the animals out?" Sadie said, surveying the store.

The screeching wheels of shopping carts and the constant whining of overtired toddlers were giving her a headache. She wished to God she'd stayed home.

"Excuse me."

A plump woman with frizzy, over-bleached hair gave Sadie an

127

apologetic look. She navigated past them, pushing a stroller occupied by a miniature screaming alien. A few feet away, she stopped, bent down and wiped something that looked like curdled rice pudding from the corner of the child's mouth.

Sadie turned to Leah. "Thank God Sam's past that stage."

At five years old—soon to be six—her son was the apple of her eye. In fact, he was the whole darned tree. A lanky imp of a boy with tousled black hair, sapphire-blue eyes and perfect bow lips, Sam was the spitting image of his mother and the exact opposite of his father in temperament. While Sam was sweet natured, gentle and loving, Philip was impatient and distant. So distant that he rarely said *I love you* anymore.

She stared at her wedding ring. *What happened to us?*

But she knew what had happened. Philip's status as a trial lawyer had grown, more money had poured in and fame had gone to his head. He had changed. The man she had fallen in love with, the dreamer, had gone. In his place was someone she barely knew, a stranger who had decided too late that he didn't want kids.

Or a wife.

"How about this?" Leah said, nudging her.

Sadie stared at the yellow dump truck. "Fill it with a stuffed bat and Sam will think it's awesome."

Her son's fascination with bats was almost comical. The television was always tuned in to the Discovery Channel while her son searched endlessly for any show on the furry animals.

"What did Phil the Pill get him?" Leah asked dryly.

"A new Leap Frog module."

"I still can't believe the things that kid can do."

Sadie grinned. "Me neither."

Sam's mind was a sponge. He absorbed information so fast that he only had to be shown once. His powers of observation were so keen that he had learned how to unlock the door just by watching Sadie do it, so Philip had to add an extra deadbolt at the top. By the time Sam was three, he had figured out the remote control and the DVD player. Sadie still had problems turning on the TV.

Sam…my sweet, wonderful, little genius.

"Maybe I'll get him a movie," Leah said. "How about *Batman Begins*?"

"He's turning six, not sixteen."

"Well, what do I know? I don't have kids."

At thirty-four, Leah Winters was an attractive, willowy brunette with wild multi-colored streaks, thick-lashed hazel eyes, a flirty smile and a penchant for younger men. While Sadie's pale face had a scattering of tiny freckles across the bridge of her nose and cheekbones, Leah's complexion was tanned and clear.

She'd been Sadie's best friend for eight years—*soul sistahs*. Ever since the day she had emailed Sadie out of the blue to ask questions about writing and publishing. They'd met at Book Ends, a popular Edmonton bookstore, for what Leah had expected would be a quick coffee. Their connection was so strong and so immediate that they talked for almost five hours. They still joked about it, about how Leah had thought Sadie was some hotshot writer who wouldn't give her the time of day. Yet Sadie had given her more. She'd given Leah a piece of her heart.

A rugged, handsome Colin Farrell look-alike passed them in the aisle, and Leah stared after him, eyes glittering.

"I'll take one of those," she said with a soft growl. "To go."

"You won't find Mr. Right in a toy store," Sadie said dryly. "They're usually all taken. And somehow I don't think you're gonna find him at Karma either."

Klub Karma was a popular nightclub on Whyte Avenue. It boasted the best ladies' night in Edmonton, complete with steroid-muscled male strippers. Leah was a regular.

"And why not?"

Sadie rolled her eyes. "Because Karma is packed with sweaty, young puppies who are only interested in one thing."

Leah gave her a blank look.

"Getting laid," Sadie added. "Honestly, I don't know what you see in that place."

"What, are you daft?" Leah arched her brow and grinned devilishly. "I'm chalking it up to my civil duty. Someone's gotta show these young guys how it's done."

"Someone should show Philip," Sadie muttered.

"Why—can't he get it up?"

"Jesus, Leah!"

"Well? Fess up."

"Later maybe. When we stop for coffee."

Leah glanced at her watch. "We going to our usual place?"

"Of course. Do you think Victor would forgive us if we went to any other coffee shop?"

Leah chuckled. "No. He'd start skimping on the whipped cream if we turned traitor. So what are you getting Sam?"

"I'll know it when I see it. I'm waiting for a sign."

"You're always such a sucker for this *fate* thing."

Sadie shrugged. "Sometimes you have to have faith that things will work out."

129

They continued down the aisle, both searching for something for the sweetest boy they knew. When Sadie spotted the one thing she was sure Sam would love, she let out a hoot and gave Leah an I-told-you-so look.

"This bike is perfect. Since his birthday is actually on Monday, I'll give it to him then. He'll get enough things from his friends at his party on Sunday anyway."

Little did she know that Sam wouldn't see his bike.

He wouldn't be around to get it.

∞ ∞ ∞

"Haven't seen you two all week," Victor Guan said. "Another day and I would've called nine-one-one."

"It's been a busy week," Sadie replied, plopping her purse on the counter. "How's business, Victor?"

"Picking up again with this cold snap."

The young Chinese man owned the Cuppa Cappuccino a few blocks from Sadie's house. The coffee shop had a gas fireplace, a relaxed ambiance and often featured local musicians like Jessy Green and Alexia Melnychuk. Not only did Victor serve the best homemade soups and feta Caesar salad, the mocha lattés were absolutely sinful.

Leah made a beeline for the washroom. "You know what I want."

Sadie ordered a Chai and a mocha.

"You see that fog this morning?" Victor asked.

"Yeah, I drove Sam to school in it. I could barely see the car in front of me."

She shivered and Victor gave her a concerned look.

"Cat walk over your grave or something?" he asked.

"No, I'm just tired of winter."

She grabbed a newspaper from the rack and headed for the upper level. The sofa by the fireplace was unoccupied, so she sat down and tossed the newspaper on the table.

The headline on the front page made her gasp.

THE FOG STRIKES AGAIN!

Her breath felt constricted. "Oh God. Not another one."

A photograph of a blond-haired, blue-eyed girl sitting on concrete steps dominated the front page. Eight-year-old Cortnie Bornyk, from the north side of Edmonton, was missing. According to the newspaper, the girl had disappeared in the middle of the night. No sign of forced entry and no evidence as to who had taken her, but investigators were sure it was the same man who had taken the others.

130

Sadie opened the newspaper to page three, where the story continued. She empathized with the girl's father, a single dad who had left Ontario to find construction work in Edmonton. Matthew Bornyk had moved here to make a better life. Not a bad decision, considering that the housing market was booming. But now he was pleading for the safe return of his daughter.

"Here you go," Victor said, setting two mugs on the table.

"Thanks," she said, without looking up.

Her eyes were glued to the smaller photo of Bornyk and his daughter. The man had a smile plastered across his face, while his daughter was frozen in a silly pose, tongue hanging out the side of her mouth.

Daddy's little girl, Sadie thought sadly.

Leah flopped into an armchair beside her. "Who's the hunk?"

"His daughter was abducted last night."

"How horrible."

"Yeah," Sadie said, taking a tentative sip from her mug.

"Did anyone see anything?"

"Nothing." She locked eyes on Leah. "Except the fog."

"Do they think it's *him*?"

Sadie skimmed the article. "There are no ransom demands yet. Sounds like him."

"Shit. That makes, what—six kids?"

"Seven. Three boys, four girls."

"One more boy to go." Leah's voice dripped with dread.

The Fog, as the kidnapper was known, crept in during the dead of night or early morning, under the cloak of a dense fog. He wrapped himself around his prey and like a fog, he disappeared without a trace, capturing the souls of children and stealing the hopes and dreams of parents. One boy, one girl. Every spring. For the last four years.

Sadie flipped the newspaper over. "Let's change the subject."

Her eyes drifted across the room, taking in the diversity of Victor's customers. In one corner of the upper level, three teenaged boys played poker, while a fourth watched and hooted every time one of his friends won. Across from Sadie, a redheaded woman wearing a mauve sweatshirt plunked away on a laptop, stopping every now and then to cast the noisy boys a frustrated look. On the lower level, one of the regulars—Old Ralph—was reading every newspaper from front to back. He sipped his black coffee when he finished each page.

"So…" Leah drawled as she crossed her long legs. "What's going on with Phil the Pill?"

Sadie scowled. "That's what I'd like to know. He says he's working long nights at the firm."

"And you're thinking, what? That he's screwing around?"

Leah never was one to beat around the bush—about anything.

"Maybe he's just working hard," her friend suggested.

Sadie shook her head. "He got home at two this morning, reeking of perfume and booze."

"Isn't his firm working on that oil spill case? I bet all the partners are pulling late nights on that one."

Sadie snorted. "Including Brigitte Moreau."

Brigitte was her husband's *right-hand-woman*, as he'd made a point of telling her often. Apparently, the new addition to Fleming Warner Law Offices was indispensable. The slender, blond lawyer, with a pair of breasts she'd obviously paid for, never left Philip's side.

Sadie wondered what Brigitte did when she had to pee.

Probably drags Philip in with her.

"It could be perfectly innocent," Leah suggested.

"Yeah, right. I was at the conference after-party. I saw them together, and there was nothing innocent about them. Brigitte was holding onto Philip's arm as if she owned him. And he was laughing, whispering in her ear." She pursed her lips. "His co-workers were looking at me with sympathetic eyes, pitying me. I could see it in their faces. Even *they* knew."

Leah winced. "Did you call him on it?"

"I asked him if he was messing around again."

Just before Sam was born, Philip had admitted to two other affairs. Both office flings, according to him. "Both meant nothing," he said, before blaming his infidelities on her swollen belly and her lack of sexual interest.

"What'd he say?" Leah prodded, with the determination of a pit-bull slobbering over a t-bone steak.

"Nothing. He just stormed out of the house. He called me from work just before you came over. Said I was being ridiculous, that my accusations were hurtful and unfair." She lowered her voice. "He asked me if I was drinking again."

"Bastard. And you wonder why I'm still single."

Sadie said nothing. Instead, she thought about her marriage.

They'd been happy—once. Before her downward spiral into alcoholism. In the early years of their marriage, Philip had been attentive and caring, supporting her decision to focus on her writing. It wasn't until she started talking about having a family that things had changed.

She flicked a look at Leah, grateful for her loyal companionship and understanding. Fate had definitely intervened when it led her to Leah.

Her friend had gone above and beyond the duty of friendship, dropping everything in a blink if she called. Leah was her life support, especially on the days and nights when the bottle called her. She'd even attended a few AA meetings with Sadie.

And where was Philip? Probably with Brigitte.

"Come on, my friend," Leah said, grinning. "I know you really want to swear. Let it out."

"You know I don't use language like that."

"You're such a prude. Philip's an ass, a bastard. Let me hear you say it. *Bas...tard.*"

"I'll let you be the foul-mouthed one," Sadie said sweetly.

"Fuckin' right. Swearing is liberating." Leah took a careful sip of tea. "So how's the book coming?"

Sadie smiled. "I finished the text yesterday. Tomorrow I'll start on the illustrations. I'm so excited about it."

"Got a title yet?"

"Going Batty."

Leah's pencil-thin brow arched. "Hmm...how appropriate."

Sadie gave her a playful slap on the arm. "It's about a little bat who can't find his way home because his radar gets screwed up. At first, he thinks he's picking up radio signals, but then he realizes he's picking up other creatures' thoughts."

"That's perfect. Sam'll love it."

"I know. I can't believe I waited so long to write something special for him."

A few months ago, Sadie decided to take a break from writing another Lexa Caine mystery, especially since her agent had secured her a deal for two children's picture books.

"It's been a welcome break," she admitted. "Lexa needed a year off. A holiday."

"Some break," Leah said. "I've hardly seen you. You've been working day and night on Sam's book."

"It's been worth it."

"Is it harder than writing mysteries?"

"Other than the artwork, I think it's easier," Sadie said, somewhat surprised by her own answer. "But then, Sam inspires me. He's my muse. Kids see things so differently."

"Wish I had one."

Sadie's jaw dropped. "A kid?"

"A muse, idiot."

Sadie grinned. "How's the steamy romance novel going?"

"I'm stumped. I've got Clara trapped below deck on the pirate ship, locked in the cargo hold with no way out."

Since the success of her debut novel, *Sweet Destiny*, Leah had found her niche and was working on her second historical romance.

"What's in the room?"

Leah gave her a wry grin. "Cases of Bermuda rum."

"Well, she's not going to drink it, so what else can she do?"

"I don't know. She can't get the crew drunk, if that's what you're thinking. "

"What if the ship caught on fire?"

Excitement percolated in Leah's eyes. "Yeah. A fire could really heat things up. Pun intended."

They were silent for a moment, lost in their own thoughts.

"Hey," Sadie said finally. "I've been tempted to cut my hair. What do you think?"

Leah stared at her. "You want to get rid of all that beautiful hair? Jesus, Sadie, it's past your bra strap." In a thick Irish accent, she said, "Have ye lost your Irish mind just a wee bit, lassie?"

"It's too much work," Sadie said with a pout.

"What does Philip think?"

"He'd be happy if I kept it long," she replied, scowling. "Maybe that's one reason why I want to cut it."

Leah laughed. "Then you go, girl."

Half an hour later, they parted ways—with Leah eager to get back to the innocent Clara and her handsome, sword-wielding pirate, and Sadie not so thrilled to be going back to an empty house. As she climbed into her sporty Mazda3, she smiled, relieved as always that she had chosen practical over the flashy and pretentious Mercedes that Philip drove.

She glanced at the clock and heaved a sigh of relief. It was almost time to pick Sam up from school.

Her heart skipped a beat.

Maybe there's been some progress today.

2

The instant Sam saw her standing in the classroom doorway, he let out a wild yell and charged at her, almost knocking her off her feet.

"Whoa there, little man," she said breathlessly. "Who are you supposed to be? Tarzan?"

"We just finished watching Pocahontas," a woman's voice called out.

"Hi, Jean," Sadie said. "How are things today?"

Jean Ellis taught a class of children with hearing impairments.

"Same as usual," the kindergarten teacher replied. "No change, I'm afraid."

Sadie tried to hide her disappointment. "Maybe tomorrow."

She studied Sam, who could hear everything just fine.

Why won't he speak?

"Did you have a good day, honey?"

Ignoring her, Sam pulled on a winter jacket and stuffed his feet into a pair of insulated boots.

"It was a great day," Jean said, signing as she spoke. "Sam made a friend. A real one this time."

Sadie was astounded. Sam's first real friend. Well, unless she counted his invisible friend, Joey.

"Hey, little man," she said, crouching down to gather him in her arms. "Mommy missed you today. But I'm glad you have a new friend. What's his name?"

When Sam didn't answer, Sadie glanced at Jean.

"Victoria," the woman said with a wink.

Grinning, Sadie ruffled Sam's hair. "Okay, charmer. Let's go."

With a quick wave to Jean, she reached for Sam's hand. She was always amazed by how perfectly it fit into hers, how warm and soft his skin was.

Outside in the parking lot, she unlocked the car and Sam scampered into the booster seat in the back. She leaned forward, fastened his seatbelt, then kissed his cheek. "Snug as a bug?"

He gave her the thumbs up.

Pulling away from the school, she flicked a look in her rearview mirror. Sam stared straight ahead, uninterested in the laughing children who waited for their parents to arrive. Her son was a shy boy, a loner who unintentionally scared kids away because of his inability to speak.

His lack of desire to speak, she corrected.

∞ ∞ ∞

Sam hadn't always been mute.

Sadie had taught him the alphabet at two. By the age of three, he was reading short sentences. Then one day, for no apparent reason, Sam stopped talking.

Sadie was devastated.

And Philip? There were no words to describe his erratic behavior. At first, he seemed mortified, concerned. Then he shouted accusations at her, insinuating so many horrible things that after a while, even she began to wonder. During one nasty exchange, he had grabbed her, his fingers digging into her arms.

"Did you drink while you were pregnant?" he demanded.

"No!" she wailed. "I haven't had a drop."

His eyes narrowed in disbelief. "Really?"

"I swear, Philip."

He stared at her for a long time before shaking his head and walking away.

"We have to get him help," she said, running after him.

Philip swiveled on one heel. "What exactly do you suggest?"

"There's a specialist downtown. Dr. Wheaton recommended him."

"Dr. Wheaton is an idiot. Sam will speak when he's good and ready to. Unless you've screwed him up for good."

His insensitive words cut her deeply, and after he'd gone back to work, she picked up the phone and booked Sam's first appointment. She didn't feel good about going behind Philip's back, but he'd left her no choice.

By the time Sam was three and a half, he had undergone numerous hearing and intelligence tests, x-rays, ultrasounds and psychiatric counseling, yet no one could explain why he wouldn't say a word. His vocal chords were perfectly healthy, according to one specialist. And he was right. Sam could scream, cry or shout. They had heard enough of *that* when he was younger.

Sadie finally managed to drag Philip to an appointment, but the psychologist—a small, timid man wearing a garish red-striped tie that screamed *overcompensation*—didn't have good news for them. He sat behind a sterile metal desk, all the while watching Philip and twitching as if he had Tourettes.

"Your son is suffering from some kind of trauma," the man said, pointing out what seemed obvious to Sadie.

"But what could've caused it?" she asked in dismay.

The doctor fidgeted with his tie. "Symptoms such as these often result from some form of...of abuse."

Philip jumped to his feet. "What the hell are you saying?"

The man's entire body jerked. "I-I'm saying that perhaps someone or something scared your son. Like a fight between parents, or witnessing drug or alcohol abuse."

Sadie cringed at his last words. The look Philip gave her was one of pure anger. And censure.

The doctor took a deep breath. "And of course, there is the possibility of physical or sexual—"

Without a word, Philip stormed out of the doctor's office.

Sadie ran after him.

He had blamed her, of course. According to him, it was her drinking that had caused her miscarriages. *And* Sam's delayed verbal development.

That night, after Sam had gone to bed, Philip rummaged through every dresser drawer. Then he searched the closet.

She watched apprehensively. "What are you doing?"

"Looking for the bottles!" he barked.

She hissed in a breath. "I told you. I am *not* drinking."

"Once a drunk..."

She cowered when he approached her, his face flushed with anger.

"It's *your* fault!" he yelled.

Guilt did terrible things to people. It was such a destructive, invisible force that not even Sadie could fight it.

∞ ∞ ∞

137

She looked in the rearview mirror and took in Sam's heart-shaped face and serious expression. She wondered for the millionth time why he wouldn't speak. She'd give anything to hear his voice, to hear one word. *Any* word. She'd been praying that the school environment would break through the language barrier.

No such luck.

Suddenly, she was desperate to hear his voice.

"Sam? Can you say Mommy?"

He signed *Mom*.

"Come on, honey," she begged. "*Muhh-mmy*."

In the mirror, he smiled and pointed at her.

Tears welled in her eyes, but she blinked them away. One day he *would* speak. He'd call her Mommy and tell her he loved her.

"One day," she whispered.

For now, she'd just have to settle for the undeniably strong bond she felt. The connection between mother and child had been forged at conception and she always knew how Sam felt, even without words between them.

She turned down the road that led to the quiet subdivision on the southeast side of Edmonton. She pulled into the driveway and pushed the garage door remote, immediately noticing the sleek silver Mercedes parked in the spacious two-car garage.

Her breath caught in the back of her throat.

Philip was home.

"Okay, little man," she murmured. "Daddy's home."

She scooped Sam out of the back seat and headed for the door. He wriggled until she put him down. Then he raced into the house, straight upstairs. She flinched when she heard his bedroom door slam.

"I guess neither of us is too excited to see Daddy," she said.

Tossing her keys into a crystal dish on the table by the door, she dropped her purse under the desk, kicked off her shoes, puffed her chest and headed into the war zone.

But the door to Philip's office was closed.

She turned toward the kitchen instead.

The war can wait. It always does.

Passing by his office door an hour later, she heard Philip bellowing at someone on the phone. Whoever it was, they were getting quite an earful. A minute later, something hit the door.

She backed away. "Don't stir the pot, Sadie."

Philip remained locked away in his office and refused to come out for supper, so she made a quick meal of hotdogs for Sam and a salad for herself. She left a plate of the past night's leftovers—ham, potatoes and

138

vegetables—on the counter for Philip.

Later, she gave Sam a bath and dressed him for bed.

"Auntie Leah came over today," she said, buttoning his pajama top. "She told me to say hi to her favorite boy."

There wasn't much else to say, other than she had finished writing the bat story. She wasn't about to tell him that she had ordered his birthday cake and bought him a bicycle, which she had wrestled into the house by herself and hidden in the basement.

"Want me to read you a story?" she asked.

Sam grinned.

She sat on the edge of the bed and nudged her head in the direction of the bookshelf. "You pick."

He wandered over to the rows of books, staring at them thoughtfully. Then he zeroed in on a book with a white spine. It was the same story he chose every night.

"My Imaginary Friend again?" she asked, amused.

He nodded and jumped into bed, settling under the blankets.

Sadie snuggled in beside him. As she read about Cathy, a young girl with an imaginary friend who always got her into trouble, she couldn't help but think of Sam. For the past year, he'd been adamant about the existence of Joey, a boy his age who he swore lived in his room. She'd often catch Sam smiling and nodding, as if in conversation. No words, no signing, just the odd facial expression. Some days he seemed lost in his own world.

"Lisa says you should close your eyes," she read.

Sam's eyes fluttered shut.

"Now turn this page and use your imagination."

He turned the page, then opened his eyes. They lit up when he saw the colorful drawing of Cathy's imaginary friend, Lisa.

"Can you see me now?" she read, smiling.

Sam pointed to the girl in the mirror.

"Good night, Cathy. And good night, friend. The end."

She closed the book and set it next to the bat signal clock on the nightstand. Then she scooted off the bed, leaned down and kissed her son's warm skin.

"Good night, Sam-I-Am."

His small hand reached up. With one finger, he drew a sideways 'S' in the air. Their nightly ritual.

"S…for Sam," she said softly.

And like every night, she drew the reflection.

"S…for Sadie."

Together, they created an infinity symbol.

She smiled. "Always and forever."

She flicked off the bedside lamp and eased out of the room. As she looked over her shoulder, she saw Sam's angelic face illuminated by the light from the hall. She shut the door, pressed her cheek against it and closed her eyes.

Sam was the only one who truly loved her, trusted her. From the first day he had rested his huge black-lashed eyes on hers, she had fallen completely and undeniably in love. A mother's love could be no purer.

"My beautiful boy."

Turning away, she slammed into a tall, solid mass. Her smile disappeared when she identified it.

Philip.

And he wasn't happy. Not one bit.

He glared down at her, one hand braced against the wall to bar her escape. His lips—the same ones that had smiled at her so charismatically the night they had met—were curled in disdain.

"You could've told me Sam was going to bed."

She sidestepped around him. "You were busy. As usual."

"What the hell's that supposed to mean?"

She cringed at his abrasive tone, but said nothing.

"You're not going all paranoid on me again, are you?" He grabbed her arm. "I already told you. Brigitte is a co-worker. Nothing more. Jesus, Sadie! You're not a child. You're almost forty years old. What the hell's gotten into you lately?"

"Not a thing, Philip. And I'll be thirty-eight this year. Not forty." She yanked her arm away, then brushed past him, heading for the bedroom.

Their marriage was a sham.

"Doomed from the beginning," her mother had told her one night when Sadie, a sobbing wreck, had called her after Philip had admitted to his first affair.

But she'd proven her mother wrong. Hadn't she? Things seemed better the year after Sam was born. Then she and Philip started fighting again. Lately, it had escalated into a nightly event. At least on the nights he came home before she went to sleep.

Philip entered the bedroom and slammed the door.

"You know," he said. "You've been a bitch for months."

"No, I haven't."

"A *frigid* bitch. And we both know it's not from PMS, seeing as you don't get that anymore."

Flinching, she caught her sad reflection in the dresser mirror. She should be used to his careless name-calling by now. But she wasn't. Each

140

time, it was like a knife piercing deeper into her heart. One of these days, she wouldn't be able to pull it out. Then where would they be? Just another statistic?

Philip waited behind her, flustered, combing a hand through his graying brown hair.

For a moment, she felt ashamed of her thoughts.

"Are you even listening to me?" he sputtered in outrage.

And the moment was gone.

She sighed, drained. "What do you want me to say, Philip? You're never home. And when you are, you're busy working in your office. We don't do anything together or go any—"

"Christ, Sadie! We were just out with Morris and his wife."

"I'm not talking about functions for the firm," she argued. "We don't see our old friends anymore. We never go to movies, never just sit and talk, never make...love."

Philip crossed his arms and scowled. "And whose fault is that? It's certainly not mine. You're the one who pulls away every time I try to get close to you. You know, a guy can only handle so much rejection before—"

"What?" She whipped around to confront him. "Before you go looking for it elsewhere?"

He stared at her for a long moment and the air grew rank with tension, coiling around them with the slyness of a venomous snake, fangs exposed, ready to strike.

When he finally spoke, his voice was quiet, defeated. "Maybe if you gave some of the love you pour on Sam to *me* once in a while, I wouldn't be tempted to look elsewhere."

He strode out of the room, his footsteps thundering down the stairs. A minute later, a door slammed.

She released a trembling breath. "Coward."

She wasn't sure if she meant Philip...or herself.

Brushing the drapes aside, she peered through the window to the dimly lit street below. It was devoid of any moving traffic, just a few parked vehicles lining the sidewalks. The faint rumble of the garage door made her clench the drapes. She heard the defiant revving of an engine, and then watched as the Mercedes backed down the driveway, a stream of frosty exhaust trailing behind it. The surface of the street shimmered from a fresh glazing of ice, and the car sped away, tires spinning on the pavement.

Philip always seemed to get in the last word.

She watched the fiery glow of the taillights as they faded into the night. Then the flickering of the streetlamp across the road caught her eye. She frowned when the light went out. One of the neighbors' dogs started barking, set off by either the abrupt darkness or Philip's noisy departure. She wasn't sure which.

And then something emerged from the bushes.

A lumbering shadow shuffled down the sidewalk, a few yards to the right of the lamp. It was a man, of that she was sure. She could make out a heavy jacket and some kind of hat, but she couldn't distinguish anything else.

The man paused across the street from her house.

Sadie was sure that he was staring up at her.

She shivered and stepped out of view, the drapes flowing back into place. When her breathing calmed, she edged toward the window again and took a surreptitious peek.

Gail, a neighbor from across the street, was walking Kali, a Shih Tzu poodle. But other than the woman and her dog, the sidewalk was empty.

Sadie locked all the doors and windows, and set the security alarm.

3

After Sadie dropped Sam off at school the next morning, she drove to Sobeys for milk and laundry detergent. Walking past the bakery section, she was flagged down by Liz Crenshaw, a vivacious food demonstrator who talked a mile a minute.

"Sadie! I was just thinking about you. How are you?"

Though the petite woman was in her early fifties, she looked closer to thirty-five. Liz had three grown children and four grandchildren who all lived back East. Without her family around to spoil, she was a sucker for Sam. And Sam adored her.

"How's your little boy doing?" Liz asked, smoothing a stray auburn curl behind one ear. "It's Sam's birthday soon, isn't it?"

Sadie tucked the milk under her arm and reached for a custard pie sample. "Monday. But his party's on Sunday. He's excited about all the birthday gifts he'll be getting."

Liz passed her a plastic spoon. "What did you get him?"

"A new bike," Sadie said between mouthfuls. "I'm not giving it to him until Monday though."

"I'd like to get him something. From Auntie Liz. What does he want, hon? Games? Books?"

Sadie grinned. "A pet bat."

The woman shuddered. "Ugh. That boy's got strange taste."

Sadie frowned at the empty sample dish in her hand, then greedily eyed the others on the stand. "Yeah, I'm trying to talk my husband into getting him a puppy as a compromise."

"Aw, I bet Sam'll love that."

"Yeah, but Philip hasn't said yes yet."

And he probably won't.

After two more samples, Sadie headed home. As she drove, she thought about Philip's relationship with Sam. He barely saw his son. Whenever he did, there was always an uncomfortable strain in the air. He never said anything to Sam, unless he wanted him to pick up something off the floor, and then Philip's voice was always so intolerant. And he never played with Sam. He was always too busy, or he didn't want to wrinkle his shirt or get his pants dirty.

She let out a sigh. She'd give anything to see Philip on the floor beside his son, both of them playing with dinosaurs or action figures—anything.

Entering the house, she headed straight for the kitchen and put the milk jug in the fridge. In the laundry room, she started a load of darks and threw the whites into the dryer. The morning passed quickly as she lost herself in her regular routine of housework.

After a bite to eat, she sat down at the small desk in the corner of the living room. She pulled out some watercolor paper and began drafting the cover for Going Batty. By two o'clock, she had created outlines of the cover and the first four pages.

"Looking good," she murmured.

She packed away the drawings and began straightening the pillows on the two sofas. Flicking a look around the room, she scowled at its stark white simplicity. She had wanted to decorate the spacious room with fresh flowers and colorful prints. But Philip wouldn't have it. He liked things the way they were. Everything in its place, no frivolous touches. The only room she'd been allowed free reign was Sam's.

The phone rang. It was her agent in Calgary.

"Hey, Jackson," she said. "I thought you'd forgotten me."

There was a feigned gasp on the other end. "I could never do that. You're a Starr, remember?"

Starr Literary Agency, run by Toronto native Jackson Starr, was giving the bigwigs in New York a run for their money.

"Any word on the conference tour?" she asked.

"That's why I'm calling. I have you booked in five cities in September, including the Crime Writers Conference in Toronto and Criminal Minds at Work in New York."

She grinned into the phone. "How rich did you make me?"

"Five thousand, plus hotel and travel expenses."

"Well, that made my day. Thanks."

"Any time. I'll deposit the check into your account this afternoon." There was a ruffle of paper. "So when you coming to visit us?"

Sadie gaze was drawn to Philip's office door. He was at work, but she still felt his presence, his disapproval. He didn't like Jackson, was jealous of him.

"Sorry, Jackson. I won't be able to get away for a bit. Maybe when I finish Sam's book."

"How's it coming?"

She filled him in on her progress, then hung up.

The thought of the extra money in her private account elated her. Philip maintained control over most of their money, which he had tied up in investments. He gave her a weekly household allowance with the agreement that any money she made would be used for Sam's basic expenses and her own. Thank God, she made a decent income. Maybe this summer they could finally go to Disneyland.

Thoughts of a family vacation, sunshine, castles and rides filled her mind and she practically danced into the laundry room. When the third load was dry, she folded Sam's clothes and placed them in a basket, along with a pair of Philip's socks that she'd discovered behind the laundry hamper. Gripping the basket under one arm, she trudged upstairs.

In the master bedroom, she opened the top drawer of the tallboy dresser and tried to ignore the five airplane bottles of alcohol that clinked together. Philip had made a halfhearted attempt to hide them under his long johns.

Five bottles, five drinks.

She tossed the socks in and slammed the drawer shut. Then she moved into the hallway, hesitating outside the door to Sam's bedroom. She wasn't sure why, but when her hand touched the brass doorknob, the hair on the back of her neck stood up. With a nervous laugh, she turned the knob and stepped inside.

A quick survey of Sam's room told her that nothing was out of the ordinary, so she set the laundry basket on the bed, next to a Batman t-shirt that had been tossed on the pillow.

She sniffed the shirt. "Clean."

Folding it, she placed it on top of the clothes in the basket. Then she gathered up the toy T-rex, raptors and pterodactyls that were scattered on the floor and put them in the treasure chest. A few minutes later, Sam's clothes had been put away in the dresser, with the exception of an Oilers jacket.

She moved toward the closet, the jacket in hand.

Ssss...

The sound brought her to a halt.

"Get a grip. What would Philip say if he saw you?" She laughed derisively. "He'd say you're being a stupid fool."

She hauled the door open.

The closet was a jumble of toys and clothes. On the floor, jammed between two stuffed animals, a red balloon left over from the Valentine's Day parade hissed at her mockingly.

As it deflated, she echoed the sound. "Idiot."

She hung up the jacket, tossed the balloon in the garbage and went downstairs. An hour later, she headed out to pick up Sam, the balloon long forgotten.

∞ ∞ ∞

"It's Friday," she said as they left the school. "Park day."

Sam let out a whoop, his mouth lined with orange Kool-Aid.

She frowned. "We have to wash that face before Daddy sees."

They crossed the parking lot and followed the sidewalk to the playground. A light blanket of snow still covered the grass, but that didn't deter the dozen or so children that played in the park.

She settled Sam on a swing and closed her fingers over his.

"Hold on tight, honey. Don't let go."

She gave the swing a gentle push. Then another.

Sunlight danced in Sam's black hair and he closed his eyes and leaned backward. He rose higher and higher, pumping his legs in delight. One of his boots slipped off and landed a few yards away. Sam didn't even notice.

"You're flying," Sadie said, grinning. "Like a bat, Sam."

Watching him, she had a sudden urge to freeze the moment, savor it forever. Times such as these made her wish she had brought a camera.

She heard his soft giggle. It built slowly, then exploded into a bout of contagious laughter.

Even the young mother next to her couldn't help but smile.

"He's having a good time," the woman said.

Sadie nodded. "Oh, to be young and carefree."

"You got that right—Andrew!"

Distracted by the antics of a lanky, freckle-faced boy climbing on top of the covered slide, the woman rushed off, leaving her daughter—still a toddler—in the baby swing next to Sam.

Sadie stared after her in disbelief. What on earth was the woman thinking? How could she leave her daughter with a complete stranger after a girl had been kidnapped?

Her gaze drifted over the school park.

A cluster of mothers chatted at a picnic table, while an olive-skinned

146

boy of about four wandered precariously close to the busy parking lot. A few feet away, an older boy—maybe thirteen—pushed a chubby girl off the steps to the slide, and a toddler of indiscriminate gender played in the sandbox, feasting on gourmet dirt laced with God knows what else. And all of that, ignored by the women at the table.

The child in the baby swing let out a soft cry.

Shaking her head in frustration, Sadie slowed Sam's swing. As she helped him down, she was torn between wanting to take him home and not wanting to leave the little girl alone.

Huge brown eyes captured hers. "Mama?"

Sadie sensed her fear. "Your mommy will be back soon."

The girl whimpered, her eyes pooling with tears.

A few minutes later, the mother rushed over. "Jeez, you'd think he'd been killed, the way he was carrying on." She nudged her head in the direction of the freckled boy.

Sadie's lips thinned. "Your daughter was getting worried."

The young woman's eyes widened as she let out a coarse snicker. "Daughter? She's not my kid. Neither of 'em are. I'm their nanny."

Sadie was shocked. "Their nanny?"

"Hey, people mistake me for their mom all the time," the woman said, as though motherhood were nothing more than a badge one could buy at the local Dollar Store.

While the woman helped the toddler from the swing, Sadie gave her a disparaging look and bit back a reply. Without another word, she took Sam's hand and led him back to the car.

"Snug as a bug," she said, clicking his seatbelt into place.

She climbed into the driver's seat. As she reached for the door, something made her look across the street.

A lone man wearing reflective sunglasses and a cowboy hat pulled low over his face waited in a gray sedan with the window rolled halfway down. She couldn't make out his features, but she did see the proud smile on his face as he watched his son or daughter playing in the park.

I wish Philip would take the time to bring Sam here.

She backed out and eased toward the parking lot exit.

That's when she noticed the man in the car again. He wasn't looking toward the playground anymore. His shadowed gaze was directed at her. Passing the man, she was relieved when he looked away.

4

"Give me a call and let me know if you'll be home for supper," Sadie said in response to Philip's voice mail greeting.

Despondent, she hung up the phone.

It was almost six and she needed to talk to him—before things got further out of hand.

Maybe therapy would help.

She let out a huff.

The day Philip went for any kind of counseling would be the day that pigs, sheep *and* cows flew.

A dull *thump* came from Sam's room.

"Honey, you okay?"

She listened at the bottom of the stairs, but he wasn't crying, so she strolled back into the living room.

The phone rang. "Hello?"

All she heard was breathing—heavy breathing.

She hung up. She'd been getting a lot of crank calls lately.

The phone rang a second time.

She picked it up. "Hello?"

More breathing.

"Is anyone there?" She sighed, irritated by the silence. "Is that the best you can do?" When there was still no response, she said, "I hope this is as good for you as it is for me."

A hooting laugh erupted on the other end.

"Leah," she muttered.

"Hey, Sadie," her friend said with a snort. "What've you got planned for tonight?"

"I'm not sure. I was hoping Philip would be home early for a change. What about you?"

"I need to get out. My neighbor has a party every Friday night and I swear they're going to come through the ceiling any minute. Of course, it wouldn't be so bad if they invited me."

Sadie heard the frustration in Leah's voice.

"Why don't you come here for supper then?" she said.

"You don't mind?"

"Of course not, you twit." *But Philip might.*

Although she'd never say *that* to Leah—even though her friend already knew that Philip wasn't her number one fan. He had issues with Leah. He didn't agree with her lifestyle, her fashion, or her influence on Sadie. He'd been trying for years to get Sadie to hook up with some of the wives from the firm. It would look good for him.

"Well…" Leah drawled, pretending to ponder the offer of free food. "Okay, I'll come over. I'll be there in twenty minutes. But as soon as Phil the Pill shows up, I'm outta there. Got it?"

"Got it."

"What's for dinner anyway?"

Sadie smiled. "Sam's favorite."

"KD?" Leah whined.

"No," Sadie said, chuckling. "His other favorite. KFC."

"Awesome! I'll be there in ten."

Leah showed up at the door wearing a pair of tight black pants that flared at the ankles and a flamboyant gypsy-style blouse in colorful bronzes and silver trim.

"Hey, it's Friday night," she said when she saw Sadie's raised brow. "I'm going out later. Now, where's the man of the house?"

"Sam! Auntie Leah's here!"

A ball of energy flew down the stairs and landed in her friend's outstretched arms.

Leah groaned. "You're getting big, buddy."

Sam looked up at Leah and a devilish grin developed.

"Tomorrow you'll be six," she said, kissing his cheek.

"Well, officially he's six on Monday," Sadie reminded her.

Leah lifted a slim shoulder. "Semantics." She set Sam down. "Are you excited for your birthday?"

He nodded, then giggled and raced back upstairs.

"Supper'll be here soon," Sadie said, heading for the kitchen.

Leah followed her. "I take it the esteemed legal eagle isn't back yet?"

"No."

"You still thinking he's—"

Sadie's prickly gaze halted her.

"Ah…" Leah murmured. "You know, until you have proof, I wouldn't get too hung up on this idea. For all you know it could be perfectly innocent."

Sadie made a sour face.

"Or you could be right," Leah added quickly.

"I don't know what to do."

"You gotta talk to the man. But be prepared. You might not like what you hear." Leah's voice softened. "God, you don't deserve—"

The doorbell rang.

"Chow's here," Sadie said, grateful for the interruption.

She headed for the living room, grabbed a couple of twenties from her purse and opened the front door. An attractive older man wearing a damp hooded raincoat stood on the porch. He held a paper bag in one hand and the bill in the other.

"Thanks," she said, handing him the money. "Hey, where's Trevor?"

The man smiled. "You must get a lot of chicken if you know us guys by name."

"My son is hooked on KFC."

The man nodded and passed her the bag. "Trevor's in the hospital getting his appendix out."

"Ouch. Hope he gets better soon."

"Yeah, well, you have a good night," he said.

As she closed the door, Leah snickered behind her.

"He was *so* checking you out, Sadie."

Sadie blushed. "I think he was checking *you* out, my friend."

"Nope. He was disappointed to see me here. Gee, should we arm wrestle for him?"

"I'm married."

Leah gave her a hard stare. "Married, maybe. But you ain't dead, sistah friend."

"You know I won't do *that*. I made a vow to Philip and I intend on keeping it. Even if he doesn't."

"I admire you for that, Sadie. So should your husband."

After supper, Leah tucked Sam into bed, leaving Sadie to tidy up. When she was finished, she stared at the phone. Philip still hadn't called.

"I think he just pulled in," Leah said behind her.

A few minutes later, Philip walked into the house. Ignoring Sadie, he tossed his briefcase on the dining room table and sent an irritated look in Leah's direction.

"What's for supper?" he asked, eyes flashing.

"KFC," Sadie replied. "It's in the fridge."

His mouth thinned as he eyed Leah, his disapproving gaze moving from her head to her feet and back up again. "What, another sleazy party tonight?"

"Nope," Leah said dryly. "Not unless *you* know where a good one is."

"Aw, bite me."

"I would, Phil, but I don't eat pork."

Philip's eyes narrowed and he strode out of the kitchen.

"Time for me to go, Sadie," Leah said, chagrined. "I feel a storm a brewin'. Sorry, hon."

"*I'm* sorry. I don't know why he has to be so rude to you."

"He's jealous of our friendship. But no worries. We're friends for life. Right?"

Sadie hugged her. "For life."

∞ ∞ ∞

As she changed into an oversized t-shirt for bed, Sadie threw a hesitant glance in Philip's direction. He'd hardly said a word to her since Leah had left. No, "How was your day, Sadie?" Or, "What did you do today?"

"Any new developments in your case?" she asked hesitantly.

Philip grunted as he peeled off his pants. "You know I can't discuss it."

Then talk to me about something else.

She tried again. "Sam had a great day at school today."

Philip paused in the doorway to the bathroom. "Did he say something?"

She bit her bottom lip and shook her head.

"Then he didn't have a great day," he said with a scowl.

When the bathroom door closed behind him, she slumped on the edge of the bed. She didn't understand what was going on with him. Why was he so distant, so cruel?

Sliding between the cool sheets, she stared at the spackled ceiling, wondering how much more indifference she could take. Philip had always been driven by his passion for success. He handled multinational corporate trials with ease, winning his fair share of high-profile cases. He kept long hours and often slept on the sofa bed in his office.

Or so he said.

The bathroom door creaked.

She rolled away, just before Philip turned off the lamp and climbed into bed beside her. A whiff of floral perfume emanated from his body. The perfume wasn't hers. It had traces of honeysuckle. Sadie hated honeysuckle.

Feigning sleep, she waited for his breathing to slow. Or for the snoring to begin. For a long moment, she wondered whether she should say something. Then she felt heavy breathing in her ear, and a hand fumbled beneath the t-shirt and stroked her thigh.

"I need you to help me with a little problem, Sadie."

You haven't needed me for a long time, she itched to say. *Now you want sex? What about my needs?*

"I need to talk," she said when Philip reached higher.

His hand froze. "What about?"

"You know what. I think we need help."

He snatched his hand away as if her words had burned him.

"If you want to see a shrink, go see one."

"Both of us," she insisted.

The mattress shifted.

She sat up, turned on the lamp.

Philip stood beside the bed, wearing nothing but a rapidly dwindling erection. He sent her a piercing stare, glaring at her as though she had lost her mind.

Had she?

"I don't need a goddamn shrink, Sadie. I'm not the one with the problem."

"Our marriage is in trouble," she said, scrambling from the bed. "We need counseling. If you won't do it for me, then at least do it for Sam's sake. Please!"

"Sam's sake? Jesus Christ, Sadie! Everything lately has been for Sam's sake. We moved out of the apartment into this house for him. Now I have to drive almost an hour instead of fifteen minutes to get to the off—"

"That apartment wasn't suitable for raising a child."

Philip stabbed a finger in the air. "*You* once thought it was the perfect place for us. Until your meddling friend got her nose out of joint."

"What's that supposed to mean? Leah had nothing to do with why I wanted to leave that apartment."

"She's changed you, Sadie. So has Sam. If you can't see that..." He shrugged.

She stared at him, baffled. "Of course having a child changed me. What did you expect? There's someone else to consider now, not just the

152

two of us."

Philip's jaw flinched, but he remained silent.

"My God," she whispered. "You're jealous of him? Of Sam?"

Philip let out an angry huff, grabbed a pillow and stalked toward the door. "I am *not* jealous of my son. I just don't like the changes I see in you." Cursing, he stormed out of the room.

"And I don't like the changes I see in you," she mumbled, slumping on the bed. *Why am I still with him?*

That was a stupid question, of course. She stayed because of Sam. Because a small part of her still believed that Philip could change. *Would* change.

She recalled the night her life began to crumble.

"I don't want kids," he'd told her. "I'm happy with the way things are. I don't understand why you'd want to jeopardize everything."

"What would be jeopardized?" she'd asked, stunned. "You'd still have your career and I'd have mine. But I want children too."

"Well, I don't."

That was the end of that discussion.

Believing he'd change his mind and feeling she had no other choice, she secretly went off the pill. Bad move. When Philip discovered the unopened prescription box, he refused to speak to her for the rest of the day. A week later, she found out she was pregnant. She was ecstatic. Philip was pissed. He screamed at her, calling her a conniving bitch.

She miscarried the next day.

Yeah, they'd been the happy couple, the envy of all their friends, especially the ones who thought Sadie and Philip had everything. They didn't realize that she was putting on a façade. In public, she'd smile and tell everyone that things were wonderful. However, in private…

There was no denying it. She was a miserable mess.

It started with the occasional drink before bed. To calm her nerves since Philip was always late. But one drink became two. Then three. Before she knew it, she started drinking during the day, hiding bottles where Philip would never find them.

A second miscarriage sent her into a bout of severe depression and she was sure she was being punished, that she'd never have a baby. She spent most nights with her other 'best friend'—a bottle of rum.

Then Philip started staying out later and later.

Her life changed forever the night he was promoted to partner. At a special banquet, a new partner and his wife were celebrating the arrival of a baby boy. The attention they received and the accolades from the senior law partners made Philip reconsider the idea of children. Suddenly, having a child seemed the perfect way to elevate his social and

153

professional status.

A year later, Sam was born.

Sadie had quit drinking the moment she found out she was pregnant. It had been rough at first, but with Leah's help and Sam as the reward, she'd fought all her demons and won.

She'd been sober ever since.

∞ ∞ ∞

As she slipped into bed, she clamped her eyes shut, blocking off tears that threatened to escape. She was not going to cry. Not over Philip.

Outside, a dog barked.

"I guess a puppy for Sam is out of the question then."

It seemed as though she had just closed her eyes, when the sound of breaking glass woke her. A piercing scream sent her heart racing and she flew out of bed.

When she left her bedroom, the first thing she noticed was the chill that swept down the hall. The second thing she saw was Sam's half-open door.

She pushed it. *"Jesus!"*

Her son's bedroom blasted her with frigid air. When she glanced toward the far wall, she spotted the culprit. The blinds were wide open and the window was shattered. On the floor, a foot from Sam's bed, was a brick.

"What's going on?" Philip demanded, flicking on the light.

Speechless, she reached a hand to her throat as her eyes swept over the room, then screeched to a stop on Sam's bed.

His *empty* bed.

Panic seared through her, hot and fearful. "Sam?"

Behind her, the closet door creaked. She moved closer, but Philip beat her to it. When he whipped it open, she was overwhelmed by relief. Her sweet boy was curled up in the corner, tears flooding his face.

She swept Sam into her arms. "Only my bat boy would hide in the closet," she murmured, stoking his hair. "Philip, who would do such a thing?"

"Shit, I don't know. Probably just kids out carousing. Tuck Sam back into bed and we'll clean this up."

"I'll put him in our bed," she said dryly. "He's not sleeping in here tonight."

"Fine. I guess I'll clean up the glass then."

Sadie hefted Sam to her hip and made for the door. She could feel

154

his heart beating rapidly, and it didn't slow until she reached her bedroom and tucked him into the king-sized bed. When he reached up, she kissed his forehead. "No worries. You're safe, honey. I promise."

Lugging the vacuum behind him, Philip paused in the doorway. His gaze wouldn't meet hers.

"I'll report it first thing in the morning," he said before disappearing.

A minute later, the vacuum roared to life.

These were the moments—although rare—that reminded her of why she had married Philip. He always took care of business.

5

Leah arrived just after one-thirty on Sunday afternoon.

Sadie took one look at her friend's downcast face and knew instinctively that something was wrong.

"What?" she demanded.

"They didn't have your cake order, Sadie."

"But I called it in last week. How could they—" She caught sight of Leah's sly grin and twinkling eyes. "What's going on?"

"April Fools!"

Leah darted down the sidewalk, then returned a minute later bearing a sweet gift. Sam's Batman birthday cake.

"April Fools' Day ends at noon, you know," Sadie muttered.

"Not in Canada, silly. Besides, I couldn't resist."

Sadie gave her a saccharine smile. "No problem. I'll get you back next year."

Juggling the cake box, Leah kicked off her shoes and made a beeline for the kitchen. "There's no room in the fridge."

"Leave it on the counter then," Sadie said, emptying a bag of steaming microwave popcorn into a bowl. "Are you ready for this?"

"It's a kids' party. How bad can it get?"

Sadie opened her mouth, but then clamped it shut. Leah didn't have kids.

And after today, she'll be very thankful of that fact.

When they entered the living room, it was already in a state of chaos. Toys and kids were scattered on every piece of furniture. In one corner, twin boys jumped on the sofa, fighting over a plastic sword. Victoria, Sam's new school friend, stood nearby with her hands on her

156

hips.

"Stop it!" the little girl demanded. "Put that down and stop fighting!" Her blond pigtails bounced with every word.

In the middle of the room, a copper-haired boy sat on the floor, eyes glued to a movie. Beside him, Sam was busy pretending to be a T-rex, his voice competing with the screams of his friends and the deafening volume of the TV. So far, he was in the lead.

The look of sheer horror on Leah's face was almost comical.

"Oh...my...God," she said. "How on earth are you gonna survive all these monsters?"

Sadie grinned and passed her the popcorn bowl. "That's what I have you for."

Leah's face paled. "Hey, you only asked me to pick up the cake. You never said anything about me staying."

"Then you don't get any cake."

"But that's...blackmail!" Leah sputtered. "Fine then, but I'm leaving after the ice cream."

The doorbell rang.

Sadie wiped her fingers on a dishcloth and hurried to the front door. When she opened it, she was relieved to see that the entertainment Philip hired had arrived.

Clancy the Clown stood on the porch, his curly orange hair flapping in the wind. His face was caked with white paint and a bulbous red nose covered his own. An exaggerated crimson smile took up the lower half of his face. To Sadie, it seemed more grotesque than happy.

"Hey, Mrs. O'Connell," the man said in a nasally tone. "Sorry I'm late. My car broke down and—"

She waved him inside. "Don't worry about it. I'm just thankful you made it. You look very...uh...colorful."

The clown sported a blue and orange striped jacket, a white shirt and bright yellow baggy pants held up by lime green and gold suspenders. A tiny top hat was perched on his head and a huge daisy was pinned to the left lapel.

Sadie suspected that one sniff would get her drenched.

"Do you want cash or a check?" she asked.

"Cash, if you have it."

She pulled a wad of twenties from her pocket. She counted out three hundred dollars, paused, then added an extra forty.

You'd better be worth it, Clancy.

Handing him the money, she said, "Three hours, right?"

The clown nodded, placing the bills inside a canvas bag. "I'll let myself out at..." He checked his watch. "Five-fifteen. Then you're on

157

your own."

"Gee, thanks."

Clancy smiled. "Did you call the agency?"

"I've had my hands full with these kids."

The crimson smile stretched further. "The boss doesn't know I'm late then. Thanks."

A snort sounded from behind Sadie.

"If you want to thank her," Leah said wryly, "then round up the little hooligans and do your thing."

The clown's brown eyes shifted to Sadie. "No problemo. Su casa es mi casa."

With a bob of his head, Clancy and his neon red, size fourteen shoes clomped into the living room. He was welcomed by a boisterous Sam who shrieked with delight.

"Oh, Jesus," Sadie moaned.

"Just think how loud things'll be when Sam starts talking," Leah said. "Once he starts, you won't be able to shut him up."

"That will be the best day of my life."

Leah's expression grew sad. "I know."

Sadie watched Sam and his friends play with Clancy. The kids were fascinated by the clown, pulling on his suspenders and stepping on his huge shoes, and shrieking when he sprayed them with the daisy.

"Hey," Leah said, jabbing her. "Let's grab a glass of chocolate milk. I need something to wash down this popcorn. "

As Sadie followed her into the kitchen, she peered over her shoulder. Sam's beaming face brought a smile to her own.

"You're a lucky mama," Leah said softly.

"I know. Sam is the best thing in my life."

∞ ∞ ∞

When the door closed behind the last child, Sadie and Leah released a collective sigh, looked at each other and laughed.

"Birthdays were way easier when he was a baby," Sadie said.

Leah pushed back her limp hair. "I just have one thing to say to you, my friend. I'm going to have a root canal this time next year. It'll be a slice of heaven compared to this."

"If you can get a two for one special I'll come with you."

"Yeah, but that would mean Phil would have to actually show up," her friend said sourly.

The smile on Sadie's face faded.

"Hey," Leah said. "I'm sure he's got a good reason for not making his own kid's birthday party."

Sadie raised a brow. "You think?"

"Well, he must have. He may be a jerk to me and treat you like crap most of the time...but he loves Sam."

"I know, but sometimes I think he loves himself more."

"Well, cheer up," Leah said, eying the mess in the room. "Sam's party was a complete success."

Sadie slumped into a chair. "Yeah. Thank God for Clancy. He did a great job keeping the kids entertained. I was so busy in the kitchen trying to get those darned sparklers to light that I didn't even see him leave."

"And lucky you, you get to do it all over again tomorrow."

"Yeah, the family birthday party. You'll be here, right?"

"Wouldn't miss it. Sam'll be so happy when he sees that bike you got him."

"I'm going to take him to the park to practice on it next weekend. Do you want to come?"

"Sure."

Leah disappeared into the kitchen and Sadie heard her rummage through the fridge.

"Ah-ha!" her friend called out. "The perfect year."

When she reappeared, she had two glasses of peach iced tea. She handed one to Sadie. "Drink up. Then I'll help you clean up this mess before Philip sees it."

Sadie's woeful gaze drifted around the living room. Paper plates were piled everywhere. They had somehow gone astray and hadn't made it into the garbage can that she had so thoughtfully provided next to the dining room table. Plastic cups, some half full of pop, were on every table and counter space. There were more cups than there had been kids.

"Ugh," Leah said behind her.

Sadie followed her friend's gaze.

A chocolate cake smear—so dark it almost looked like dried blood—stretched across the kitchen wall, three feet from the ground, a small handprint at the end.

"Your house is a disaster," Leah said unnecessarily.

Sadie sighed. "Well, at least it's quiet."

Sam had gone upstairs to his room, tired from all the excitement and junk food. The last time she had seen him, he was lying on his bed.

"He's probably asleep," Leah said, reading her thoughts.

Sadie gulped down her iced tea, then set to work on the kitchen, while Leah looked after the living room. After an hour had passed, all that was left to do was run the vacuum over the carpets and turn on the dishwasher.

"All done," Leah said, wiping a bead of sweat from her brow.

"Thanks. I can handle what's left."

As Sadie watched Leah climb into her car, a part of her wanted to holler, "*Come back!*"

"You're being silly," she muttered.

Sadie closed the door and slid the deadbolt into place. Then she locked up the rest of the house, set the alarm for the night and went upstairs to check on Sam.

When she opened the door to his room, she smiled. Sam was stretched out across his bed. On top of the blankets. A soft snore issued from his half-opened mouth. He had passed out from exhaustion, his face covered with chocolate cake, white, black and blue icing, and an orange pop mustache.

"Happy birthday, little man," she whispered, tucking an extra blanket around him.

She closed the door and headed downstairs to wait for Philip.

∞ ∞ ∞

Sadie was abruptly roused from a deep sleep. She jerked to a sitting position, inhaling deeply, and looked at the space beside her. It was unoccupied, the blanket still tucked under the pillow. She had waited for Philip downstairs for hours. Eventually, she had given up and gone to bed.

She peered at the bedroom clock. It was half past midnight. She'd only been asleep for about forty-five minutes. In the murky shadows of the room, she felt a foreign presence, a movement of air that was so subtle it could have been her own breath.

A draft?

She squinted at the window. It was closed.

Somewhere in the house a floorboard creaked.

Philip must be home.

Tossing the blankets aside, she slid from the bed and walked to the door. Remembering the brick thrown through Sam's window, she froze. Her stomach fluttered as she imagined a gang of teen hoodlums breaking into the house.

But the alarm would go off, silly.

Still, she pressed an ear to the door and strained to listen.

At first, there was silence. Then another creak.

"Philip," she mumbled.

She was about to open the door when she heard an unfamiliar ticking sound. Had Philip bought a clock for the hall?

She listened again.

Tick... tick, tick.

Whatever it was, it was coming closer.

Her heart began to pound a maniacal rhythm and her breath quickened. When a shadow passed underneath the door, she held her breath. Her heart thumped almost painfully in her chest.

Then the shadow was gone.

Cautiously, she opened the door. Just a crack.

The hall was empty.

And no ticking.

Maybe I dreamt it.

With a tremulous laugh, she flung open the door, a show of false bravado. Maybe Philip was working in his office. Maybe he'd gone to check on Sam.

"Philip?"

She walked down the hall and stopped in front of Sam's room. Her toes tingled as a draft teased her feet. She shivered, then opened the door.

The window that Philip had replaced gaped open—black and hungry—like a mouth waiting to be fed. The curtains flapped in the night wind, two tongues lashing out.

She frowned. Philip hadn't left the window open. He'd gone to work early, without a word to either of them. And Sam couldn't have opened it. He wasn't tall enough.

Did I leave it open?

She crossed the room, barely looking at the mound in the bed. She reached for the window and tugged it shut. The lock clicked into place, the sharp sound shattering the stillness.

Then she glanced at the bed.

Sam hadn't even stirred. But then again, he never did. He was almost comatose when he slept and nothing could wake him early, short of a sonic boom.

She tiptoed to the bed and touched his hair. Then, closing her eyes, she leaned down, kissed his warm forehead and breathed in his sweet child scent. He smelled of chocolate and sunshine.

"Snug as a bug," she whispered.

She stepped back, her foot connecting with something soft and furry. Reaching down, she fumbled in the dark until she found the stuffed toy dog that Philip had given Sam the night before. She moved quietly toward the closet, inched the door open and tossed the toy inside. Then she stepped out into the hall, shutting the bedroom door behind her.

Her gaze flitted to the far end of the hallway, where shadows danced between silk trees that stood in the alcove. Beside the trees—two-thirds up the wall—was a small oval window, and through it, a new moon was visible. It hung in the cloudless sky, a pearlescent pendant on invisible string.

It was a beautiful night, one that was meant to be shared.

Loneliness filled her, but she shrugged it off and plodded down to the kitchen to get a glass of juice. Five minutes later, she went back upstairs, with every intention of crawling into bed and ignoring the fact that Philip hadn't even bothered to call on the night of their son's birthday party.

As she passed Sam's door, a flicker of light beneath it caught her eye. Then she heard a soft thud. Sam must have fallen out of bed again. He had done that on two other occasions. Usually he woke up screaming.

She opened the door and sucked in a breath as her gaze was captured by something that made no sense at all.

The window was open again.

She blinked. "What the—?"

Moonlight streamed through the window, illuminating the bed. It was empty.

"Sam?"

She reached for the light switch.

"I wouldn't do that if I were you."

At the sound of a stranger's hoarse whisper in her son's bedroom, she did the most natural thing.

She flicked on the light.

6

A black-hooded monster held her son in his arms.

Sam wasn't moving.

The oxygen was instantly sucked from the room, making it impossible for Sadie to breathe. The glass slipped through her fingers, orange juice pooling at her feet. Speechless, she took a trembling step forward. "Please—"

"Don't move!" the stranger growled from the depths of the sweatshirt hood. "You have ten seconds to make a decision. Let me walk out of here with the kid, or your son dies." He shifted Sam's limp body in his arms and a glint of metal flashed.

A gun. It was aimed at Sam's head.

She trembled uncontrollably. *Oh Jesus...*

"Let him go," she said in a shaky voice.

He snorted, as if he found her comment amusing. When he twisted his head to glance over his shoulder at the open window, she saw a ghostly face with a hooked nose that looked like it had been broken a few times. A red smear gleamed in the crease that ran from the side of his nose to his wide, thick lips. His cheek was pale alabaster and flecked with spidery imperfections.

Pockmarks, she guessed.

The man turned, examining her just as closely. "Are you that fucking stupid? Turn off the goddamn light!"

Although her hand trembled noticeably, she obeyed.

Dressed in black, the man blended into the shadowed corner.

She hissed in a breath. "What did you do to my son?"

"Just gave him something to make him sleep." The man sighed, frustrated. "Why'd you have to go and mess things up? If you'd stayed asleep I'd be outta here already."

"I want my son," she said with a whimper. "Just let him go. Leave. I won't tell anyone. Please. Just give him to me and walk out the door."

"That ain't gonna happen."

The man did something unexpected. He moved into the moonlight, sat down on the bed and propped her son in his lap, like a ventriloquist's doll.

"Is it, Sam?" He gripped Sam's chin and turned his head from side to side. "No, Mommy," he said in an eerie, childlike voice. "I'm going with this man."

Sadie staggered against the wall. "No, he's not."

The man tossed Sam on the bed. "Shit, shit, *shit!*"

She shivered at the pure madness in his voice.

"I'll tell *you* how this is gonna play out," he muttered. "First, you're gonna promise not to leave this room for twenty minutes."

"Wait!" she cried, tears flowing down her face. "Take me instead. You don't need him. I'll come with you, do whatever you want."

"I don't need you." He stroked the gun against Sam's hair. "I have what I came for. Five seconds."

She hitched in a breath, her heart aching, burning…dying.

"You sick…*per*vert," she said between gritted teeth.

"I'm no perv."

"Then what do you want with my son?"

"For fuck's sake, shut up! You've already screwed things up enough. No one's ever seen me. No one!"

That's when it hit her.

The Fog.

She shrank back against the wall. "I won't let you take my son."

The Fog laughed mockingly. "You won't *let* me?"

She stood slowly, quivering from head to toe. "No. I won't."

In a flash, she lunged for the gun. The man backhanded her across the face. Pain exploded in her left temple. Enraged, she roared and hurled herself at him again. This time she managed to dislodge the gun from his hand.

She dove for it.

He kicked her in the ribs. "Stupid bitch."

Forcing her away from the gun, he kicked her again. And again. Then he reached down, hauled her up by her hair and flung her across the room. A sharp twinge pierced her side as she landed with a sickening thud against the dresser. She let out a pained gasp. When she looked up, Sam was lying helpless in the man's arms.

"I'm walking out of here," The Fog said. "With the kid. And you're not gonna stop me. You know why?"

She shook her head, unable to move or speak.

"Because if you try to stop me..." He pressed the gun to Sam's head and pretended to pull the trigger. *"Bam!"*

"I can give you money," she cried out. "I've got twenty-five thousand in my checking account."

He sneered. "Is that all he's worth to you?"

"I'm begging you...a *hundred* thousand! Whatever you want, I'll get it. Please! Just tell me how much you want."

The Fog tossed Sam over his shoulder with the ease of someone hefting a sack of potatoes. Then he strode toward her and leaned down, his shadowed face bare inches from hers.

"What I *want* is to see nothing in the papers," he said, his breath a simmering stew of cigarettes, onions and beer. "No description, no nothing. I want you to go back to bed and pretend you never seen me."

"I can't do that."

"Yes, you can. And you will."

"But the police—"

"Fuck the police! You want your kid to live?"

Sadie shuddered. "Yes, I want Sam to live."

"Don't leave this room for twenty minutes."

She stretched out a trembling hand. "Don't take my baby."

The Fog straightened. Then he yanked the door open and the light from the hall illuminated him for a brief moment.

"Please," she wept.

"Please," he mimicked scornfully. "You're pathetic."

She closed her eyes in agreement. Then, in a last ditch effort, she clawed her way across the floor, writhing in agony as a hot wave threatened to pull her under.

The Fog watched her, his thin lips twisting into a sinister smile. "I see one description—you even say you saw me—and I'll send the kid back to you all right. In little *bloody* pieces. You got that?"

She couldn't answer.

"Two seconds!" he snapped, raising the gun to Sam's head.

"Okay! Take him! Just please...don't hurt him."

Then Sadie did the only thing she could do. She let a madman take her son.

Alone, she cried in the dark, scared to move, scared not to.

"God help me," she sobbed. "Help Sam!"

But God wasn't listening.

165

Philip stumbled into the house at one fifteen. And *stumbled* was an understatement. Upstairs in Sam's room, Sadie heard the sound of glass hitting the floor. It was followed by a belligerent curse.

She stared at the bat signal clock on Sam's wall.

The twenty minutes were up. Five minutes ago. They had passed slowly, like a never-ending funeral dirge for the Pope. She had mentally shut down and collapsed on Sam's bed in a haze of overwhelming pain, grief and guilt.

She pulled herself to her feet, ignoring the throbbing spasms in her ribs. Her legs shook, her heart raced and her head pounded.

What do I do? What do I tell Philip?

She moaned. "Oh, God. Sam…"

She stepped out into the hall, one hand on the doorframe for support. Her throat burned as heavy footsteps lumbered up the stairs.

Philip turned the corner and lurched to a stop when he saw her. "Sadie?" he slurred. "Whatcha doing? Waiting up for me?"

"Philip, I n-need—"

"I need you to blow me." He grinned lecherously and tried to grab her.

She batted his arm away. "Philip, stop it!"

"So I'm a little drunk," he said, pouting. "We can still—"

"Sam's gone," she whispered. "He took Sam."

"What?"

"The Fog…took…him, Philip." Her voice caught in the back of her throat as deep, wracking sobs hiccupped to the surface.

Philip stared at her. "What the hell are you talking about?" He pushed her aside and staggered into Sam's room. "Sam's sleeping in his—"

He stopped, confused. Then he strode to the closet and flung the door open. "Where is he, Sadie?" He whipped around, almost colliding into her. "What've you done with my son?"

She was stunned. "I haven't done anything, Philip. I told you, Sam's been kidnapped."

"Kidnapped?" His glazed eyes went immediately sober and his face blanched. "Oh shit." He looked as though someone had sucker punched him in the gut.

She moved slowly toward their bedroom.

"What are you doing?" he demanded, following her.

"Calling the police."

"You haven't called them yet?"

She reached for the cordless phone. "I just...found him gone."

Philip sank down on the bed and watched her dial.

When the 911 operator answered, Sadie's composure crumbled. "My son's been kidnapped," she wept into the phone.

The man took her information, then instructed her not to hang up. "The police will be there soon."

Phone in hand, she stood by the window and stared at the street below. There were no signs of life. No cars, no lights.

No Sam.

Then she heard the siren wailing in the distance.

"Did you see anyone?" Philip rasped.

She hesitated and swallowed hard, remembering The Fog's parting words. *'If you even say you saw me, I'll send the kid back to you all right. In little bloody pieces.'*

She believed him. If she said anything, Sam was as good as dead. And how would she live with *that* on her conscience? But she realized something else. Once she started lying, there was no turning back.

She choked back a muffled sob. "I heard something. I thought he fell out of bed. But when I went to check on him..." She stared at the phone. "Sam was gone."

The lies had begun.

Children of the Fog is available in ebook edition and will soon be available as a trade paperback

YOU HAVE 10 SECONDS TO MAKE A DECISION:
Let A Kidnapper Take Your Child, Or Watch Your Son Die.
Choose!

Children of the Fog

Sadie O'Connell is a bestselling author and a proud mother. But her life is about to spiral out of control. After her six-year-old son Sam is kidnapped by a serial abductor, she nearly goes insane. But it isn't just the fear and grief that is ripping her apart. It's the guilt. Sadie is the only person who knows what the kidnapper looks like. And she can't tell a soul. For if she does, her son will be sent back to her in "little bloody pieces".

When Sadie's unfaithful husband stumbles across her drawing of the kidnapper, he sets into play a series of horrific events that sends her hurtling over the edge. Sadie's descent into alcoholism leads to strange apparitions and a face-to-face encounter with the monster who abducted her son--a man known only as...The Fog.

"Reminiscent of *The Lovely Bones*, Cheryl Kaye Tardif weaves a tale of terror that will have you rushing to check on your children as they sleep. With exquisite prose, *Children of the Fog* captures you the moment you begin and doesn't let go until the very end." —bestselling author Danielle Q. Lee, author of *Inhuman*

"Ripe with engaging twists and turns reminiscent of the work of James Patterson, Tardif once again tugs at the most inflexible of heartstrings...*Children of the Fog* possesses you from the touching beginning through to the riveting climax." —Kelly Komm, award-winning author of *Sacrifice*

ISBN: 978-0-9866310-6-1 (trade paperback)
ISBN: 978-0-9866310-7-8 (ebook)

Available at various retailers, including Amazon, Chapters and KoboBooks

Book 1 in the Divine series by Cheryl Kaye Tardif...

Divine Intervention

CFBI agent Jasmine McLellan is assigned a hot case—one that requires the psychic abilities of the PSI Division, a secret government agency located in the secluded town of Divine, BC.

Jasi leads a psychically gifted team in the hunt for a serial arsonist—a murderer who has already taken the lives of three innocent people. Unleashing her gift as a *Pyro-Psychic*, Jasi is compelled toward smoldering ashes and enters the killer's mind. A mind bent on destruction and revenge.

Jasi's team, consisting of *Psychometric Empath* and profiler, Ben Roberts, and *Victim Empath*, Natassia Prushenko, is led down a twisting path of dark, painful secrets. Brandon Walsh, the handsome, smooth-talking *Chief of Arson Investigations,* joins them in a manhunt that takes them across British Columbia—from Vancouver to Kelowna, Penticton and Victoria.

While impatiently sifting through the clues that were left behind, Jasi and her team realize that there is more to the third victim than meets the eye. Perhaps not all of the victims were *that* innocent. The hunt intensifies when they learn that someone they know is next on the arsonist's list.

The case heats to the boiling point as Jasi steps out of the flames...and into the fire. And in the heat of early summer, Agent Jasi McLellan discovers that a murderer lies in wait...*much closer than she imagined.*

ISBN: 9781412035910 (trade paperback)
ISBN: 978-0-9865382-2-3 (ebook)

Available at various retailers, including Amazon, Chapters and KoboBooks

Check out Cheryl Kaye Tardif's terrifying thriller...

Whale Song

A haunting story that will change how you view life...and death.

Thirteen years ago, Sarah Richardson's life was shattered after the tragic death of her mother. The shocking event left a grief-stricken teen-aged Sarah with partial amnesia.

Some things are easier to forget.

But now a familiar voice from her childhood sends Sarah, a talented mid-twenties ad exec, back to her past. A past that she had thought was long buried.

Some things are meant to be buried.

Torn by nightmares and visions of a yellow-eyed wolf and aided by creatures of the Earth and killer whales that call to her in the night, Sarah must face her fears and recover her memories—even if it destroys her.

Some things are meant to be remembered—at all cost.

"Moving...[a] perennially crowd-pleasing combination of sweet and sad." —*Booklist*

"Whale Song is deep and true, a compelling story of love and family and the mysteries of the human heart...a beautiful, haunting novel." —New York Times Bestselling novelist Luanne Rice, author of *What Matters Most*

"I read Whale Song and loved it." —Jodelle Ferland, actress in *Eclipse*

ISBN: 978-0-9866310-5-4 (trade paperback)
ISBN: 978-0-9865382-7-8 (ebook)

Available at various retailers, including Amazon, Chapters and KoboBooks

Cheryl Kaye Tardif is an award-winning, bestselling Canadian suspense author. Her novels include Children of the Fog, The River, Divine Intervention, and Whale Song, which New York Times bestselling author Luanne Rice calls "a compelling story of love and family and the mysteries of the human heart...a beautiful, haunting novel."

Her next thriller, Divine Justice (book 2 in the Divine series), will be published in spring 2011, in ebook and trade paperback editions.

Cheryl also enjoys writing short stories inspired mainly by her author idol Stephen King, and this has resulted in Skeletons in the Closet & Other Creepy Stories (ebook) and Remote Control (novelette ebook).

In 2010 Cheryl detoured into the romance genre with her contemporary romantic suspense debut, Lancelot's Lady, written under the pen name of Cherish D'Angelo.

Booklist raves, "Tardif, already a big hit in Canada...a name to reckon with south of the border."

Cheryl's website: http://www.cherylktardif.com
Official blog: http://www.cherylktardif.blogspot.com
Twitter: http://www.twitter.com/cherylktardif

You can also find Cheryl Kaye Tardif on MySpace, Facebook, Goodreads, Shelfari and LibraryThing, plus other social networks.